Torment of the Divine

ORIGINAL SIN

ERIC ADAMS

Table of Contents

Prologue

"ELOHIM!!! YOU MUST RELEASE THE WEAPON NOW!!!" Sapien yells in horror to his friend. Embers from the green and yellow flames pelt his face. The once vibrant and flawless city he helped build now lies in ruins before him.

"I CAN'T! THE FAILSAFE IS NOT READY!" Elohim hollers back as he frantically tries to finish his work. The storm rages on with the sounds of forceful winds whistling through the remaining buildings and the screams of mutilated angels echoing all around.

Sapien yells to Elohim again. "THEY'RE GETTING CLOSER! IF YOU DON'T RELEASE IT NOW, WE ARE DEAD!"

"AND IF I RELEASE IT TOO SOON, ALL THIS WILL BE FOR NOUGHT!"

The howls of anger from the monstrosities the Weavers created draw nearer as they continue their progression towards the two elder angels. Elohim looks past Sapien's eclipsed figure and to the sight of the titans decimating anything that stands in their way. The emerald fires span across the horizon.

Quickly, he turns back to his work and looks at the table behind him. On top of it rests a humanoid figure in a comatose state that is made of Pure Light. It shines so brightly that Elohim needs to wear special obsidian glass goggles to be able to look at it.

"I am sorry," he whispers to it. "But we are out of time. When you wake, you must wake fighting. The Darkness will be right behind you. Fight, my child. Defeat the Darkness and bring us back."

Sapien screams in agony behind him. He turns around to see his friend getting torn apart by the black-skinned creatures. A few of them turn and lock eyes with Elohim, causing fear to run through him as though his blood cells were made of lead. He turns back around and presses the ignition button, shooting the light-being into the far reaches of the universe while simultaneously causing an explosion to happen from under him.

"Bring us back..." he exhales before everything around him is devoured by The Darkness.

Moments later, but lightyears away,

God awakens.

His eyes shutter open and shut as he looks around, trying to get his bearings. He only has time to look at his hands before he is suddenly hit by an immeasurable force and a pain unlike any other. It tears at him like a million leeches gnawing on his skin.

"AAAAHHHHH!!!" he roars in pain, causing Pure Light to radiate from inside and burn The Darkness off him. But it comes back immediately after the light dulls. God screams out again, but with purpose and force. His light grows brighter and more abundant. But again, it dulls, and the Darkness returns.

Over and over, this cycle repeats, each time the light lasts a little longer. Eventually, after what seems like an eternity, God is able to power up his Light and have it last for minutes, thus keeping the Darkness at bay. Minutes are small amounts of time in scale. But to God, minutes are lifetimes, and he uses them productively. Because all that he has had to think about these last few millennia is what he needed to create and how much time he needed to do it.

God hovers in a seated position, his legs crossed, and his back hunched forward. Strands of Pure Light run from the front of his torso and into a ball that he weaves like a spider spinning its web. He maneuvers and shapes it carefully into a being of its own. When he is satisfied with it, he floats it into the air and stares at it while rubbing his chin in thought. He ponders all cases and scenarios of what could happen when he brings his creation to life.

"It will not be as strong as I am," he says to himself after some time. "It will need to be able to defend itself."

God walks behind the being and grabs its back from between each shoulder and spine with both hands. He pulls upward and outward as far as he can reach. He then focuses on one at a time, crafting them into beautiful, feathered wings. Their quills are translucent and act as conductors of the Pure Light within the being, giving it a form of defense to shield itself with.

As he admires his work, the light around God begins to flicker, signaling that the Darkness is returning. He walks back around to the front of the being and places his hand on the center of its chest. In doing so, a wave of Pure Light cascades over the being's body.

"It is time, my son," God says warmly as the light begins to fade.

"Awaken."

Chapter
1

Let there be Light

Millenia have passed since the light-being that God created first awoke into a world of chaos. Its first sight was that of its father fending off the Darkness. God's back was to it, and not a word was spoken, yet it instinctively knew to help its father. It stepped next to God, made eye contact, and nodded at each other before pushing the darkness back in unison.

In their short periods of peace, the two discussed what would be done in the next period. More light beings would need to be made in order to have a significant chance against the Darkness. The light-being would hold off the Darkness on his own for as long as he could while his father worked on creating his siblings.

Four new light-beings came into existence. God decided to name them Angels, and together they were able to push the Darkness far enough away to create themselves a sanctuary. This sanctuary spanned the size of a galaxy, held together by large orbs of light. However, God knew that this sanctuary would not suffice forever. More Light would need to be spread in order to expel the Darkness for good.

So, he decided to send his children on similar but individual tasks while he worked towards his own. He gave each child a single seed.

Within this seed contained the power to create worlds named Gardens. The Angel's tasks were to go to different parts of the sanctuary and create their own Gardens as they best saw fit. God gave them these tasks in hopes that one of the five would create a Garden fit for the next part of his plan. He knew that this would take quite some time, so he sent his children on their ways and began focusing on his own task.

After a thousand years, the Gardens were ready, and God had made his choice as to which one was the perfect fit for his new creations. In this Garden, the trees grow tall, stretching up to the sun. Their branches reaching out but falling just short of touching the next tree. Their limbs are solid and strong, filled with hearty leaves of green. Their trunks planted firmly in the ground, incapable of being moved as a soft breeze rustles through them.

A small creek trickles like large shards of glitter reflecting in the sun as the water flows into a nearby pond. The pond waters are as transparent as freshly cured glass, allowing clear sight to the bottom. The bottom is lined with soft sediment, only broken up by clumps of grass poking through. Elegant fish swim around without worry. Their fins and tails flow with the water's current, giving the illusion that they are flying and not swimming around in circles. An apple tree sits at the pond's edge. Its bright red apples look like rubies against an emerald leaf backdrop.

Among the other beauties of flowers and shrubs is the soft, lush grass that lines the floor of the garden. The grass is golden green in color and feels like a kitten's fur. It too is being swayed by the gentle breeze that is blowing; however, it is also being parted in a zig-zag pattern. Upon closer inspection, we see a snake. But this is no ordinary serpent. This snake is grey in color with flecks of silver shimmering in the sun, almost reflective. With blue eyes as bright as a cloudless sky.

It slowly slithers through the garden towards the sound of a muffled voice. As it draws closer, the voice becomes clearer. The silver serpent climbs up to a tree branch, out of sight but within view, and observes the conversation taking place.

A man and woman stand embraced to each other in the nude. Both are looking upwards, listening to a voice that appears to be coming down from the sky. "This garden is your home. Everything you shall ever need can be found here. If you live by the commands that I have given, you will live for an eternity. Now go forth and flourish."

The serpent watches the man and woman leave through a covered path. "Magnificent," it thinks to itself.

"My Child, are you here?" The voice from the sky calls out.

The serpent slithers down from its perch and over to the spot where the man and woman had stood. As it gets there, the sun grows brighter and illuminates the garden. A large orb of white light floats down, dulling the closer it gets to the ground. The orb begins to shift and take shape, turning into a humanoid figure. There before the serpent stands God.

God is a massive being standing close to eight feet tall. He wears a white robe trimmed in gold and has a thick but trimmed snow-white beard. His hair is short but just as white as his beard, and even though he is very defined and muscular, his face is gentle yet wrinkled from millennia of thought. But his most distinctive feature is his eyes. They are like looking into a storm. Grey, clouded, and ominous.

Every living thing around him blossoms and blooms to its fullest extent from the aura that surrounds him. This is known as The Grace of God. Anything in it becomes its perfect form. A truly magnificent power.

God looks down at the snake in the grass. "It is safe, my child," he says with a smile.

The serpent coils up and begins to glow, it too starts transforming itself into a humanoid being. Its body fully illuminates as wings sprout from its back. It stands upright and spreads its wings as the glow of its body begins to fade.

Before God stands an angel. His pure white, wavy hair hangs down just touching his shoulders. His face is clean-shaven and square jawed. Although shorter than his father by about a foot, the angel matches his physique. His white feathered wings fold behind him as he kneels before God, and he too wears a white hooded robe that is also lined with gold.

God lays his hand on the angel's shoulder. "Stand." He tells him. The angel looks up at his father and begins to rise. His eyes are ice blue and piercing, but full of light and admiration of his father. God removes his hand as the angel gets to his feet and greets him with a warm smile. "How is the garden?" God asks.

"The garden grows and prospers well, father." The angel responds. God nods in acknowledgment as he walks around admiring his child's work.

The angel stares off in the direction that the man and woman had left. "Father, were those the humans?" It asks after a minute.

Again, God nods, still inspecting the garden.

"Am I to take care of them as well?"

"No, you are not," God replies softly. "They have been given their tasks. I have laid out my commandments, and they are to follow them. "You," he says as he looks at the angel, "are never to interfere with them. You are meant to simply observe them and make sure that they are carrying out their purpose."

"Their purpose, Father?" the angel asks confusingly. God stops and turns his body to him.

"Their purpose is to inherit this earth from the heavens. To do so, they must multiply and learn how to rule themselves under my law. Your task is to make sure they do so and guide them under the cover of the shadows until they are fit to do it themselves." The angel looks down at the ground. "I know the task I am giving you is a large one. They have their purpose, and I have my purpose for them. I chose you above your siblings because I knew that you were the best suited for this task." God says as he places his hands on the angel's shoulders.

The angel looks up at God. "Walk with me." God says with a smile.

The two begin to walk through the garden as God talks. "As you'll recall, I gave each of my children a garden to oversee. Each garden was started identically, by one seed. I then gave each of you the power to grow that garden however you best saw fit. Your sister's showed promise at the beginning but lacked the attention to detail that was needed. And although it was beautiful, it was messy and untamed. Not suitable for what I needed for mankind."

Your second brother's Garden, much like his own head, was very clustered. There was far too much in it, and everything was in groups according to size and coordination with one another. There was no free flow to it at all, and it felt as though I was walking through a maze." God says with a chuckle. "Your eldest brother was too precise. Everything had its place and was far too organized. He raised his garden in more of a strategic way, and I was concerned that it would have forced mankind down an already laid path. Negating their free will."

"That doesn't surprise me at all." The angel says with a grin. This makes God chuckle again. "Nor did it I." He replies while laughing. "Your smaller brother's Garden, however, rivaled yours. In fact, when it comes to beauty, the two are nearly identical. However, his was all free flow. There were no defined edges or anything that gave a sense of direction. It just simply...was."

God stops walking and turns to the angel. "That is why I chose your garden above theirs. You allowed your garden to grow freely, yet helped it remain able to flourish. You did not interfere with its growth but guided and shaped it to be the best it could be. And this is exactly what I am looking to be done with mankind." God grips the angel's shoulders and looks him in the eye. "This is why I have chosen you to oversee mankind's existence. To be their guardian angel, now and forever. My first son,"

"Lucifer."

Lucifer bows his head and kneels, and God looks down at him. "Rise. We have another matter to discuss."

Lucifer stands. "I believe that I already know what the other matter is."

God nods his head a few times in a row. "You will be alone here. Your siblings and I still have the Darkness to contend with. It will be some time until my plan with the humans will be able to be carried out with effect, but the Darkness will not wait. We still will need to keep it at bay." God pauses and looks around. "This garden must succeed Lucifer. The humans are vital to our victory over the Darkness."

Lucifer nods in agreement. "I understand."

"Then I take my leave."

God begins to glow as he begins to hover towards the sky. "Remember, Lucifer. If the humans see your angelic form, it will shatter their fragile world. The balance of light and dark would unravel, and creation itself could collapse. Under no circumstances must you reveal yourself," he says while staring intensely at his son. "Remain as the serpent, observe and guide them. Never interfere. Do you understand?"

"Yes, Father." Lucifer responds as he watches God fade in the distance.

"Thy will be done."

Chapter 2

Out of the Shadows

For nearly two years, Lucifer watched them move through the garden's endless green. By day, he slithered unnoticed, the serpent hidden among the blooms. By night, under the cover of the dark sky, he moved in closer, studying the patterns of their laughter, their arguments, their silence. He began to know their routines as if they were carved into the soil itself. This gave him the chance to stretch out and tend to the other areas of the garden that were not within the human's limits.

The garden stretched farther than the eye could follow, vast oceans glittering with life and continents rolling out like green waves. It was a world complete unto itself, an echo of Earth yet untouched by decay or shadow. It had its own weather patterns, and there were no seasons. It was fully engulfed by Pure Light. Yes, it rotated and had night and day, but being within the Light allowed for everything to remain the same, no matter what side the sun was shining on. The night provided the rest all life needed, and the day provided the growth of it all.

It was perfectly balanced.

Lucifer often wondered why the seed that God had given him to create the Garden had grown into such a vast paradise for only two souls. Yet he understood: they were meant to flourish, to spread, to fill this expanse with generations to come. However, the man and woman were unaware of the rest of the garden. To them, the world was only as big as what they could walk to during the day and be able to return to at night. They had everything that they needed within their environment.

Even though they were made through complexities that Lucifer could not yet understand, they were quite simple creatures of habit. Each morning, they would wake up, stretch, and rub their eyes. Then the man would make his way to the stream to wash his face.

He resembled God in his looks, but much younger. His hair and beard were the color of rich earth, but his skin glowed with golden light stretched across a form sculpted in the image of God. After the man was done washing himself, he would then go about his way, tending the crops he had grown. He worked hard and took his time with each plant to ensure it was sustaining properly. He dug little trenches between each row of plants that he would fill with water that he had carried with him up from the stream. He never harvested the crop too early or too late. Always just at the right moment. The man would then take the harvest back to the woman in the evenings, and the two would share a meal. Lucifer was pleased by how well the man was taking care of the garden that he had created.

The woman would start her day by heading to the pond to bathe herself. She would slip her feet in the water just to her ankles and then close her eyes while tilting her head up to feel the warmth of the sun. She would just sit there like a smooth marble statue, and everything seemed to slow down around her. The water would glisten like slow flashes of light reflecting off diamonds. The breeze would barely move her thick, raven black hair. The songs of birds seemed to fade into white noise, and the sun seemed to glow a little brighter. But once she opened her eyes, everything returned to its normal speed. As though the Garden had paused for a moment and then started back up again.

The woman would then stretch her arms above her head, press her hands together and dive into the water. She would swim straight to the bottom and brush her stomach against the soft silt before swimming back to the surface. As she broke through the water, she would swing her head back, making water cascade through the air in tiny droplets. She would then lay on her back and float in the middle of the pond. Water would drop off the front of her nubile body, then return to its source. Her body is toned and curvy, and her skin is sun-kissed but pale. Her hair rests at her lower back when dry, and is thick, full and sways when she walks.

However, her most stunning feature would have to be her eyes. They are pale green with hints of yellow, surrounded by a thin black outline. Her pupils are blacker than the deepest pits, rivaling the darkest parts of the universe that have never been touched by the sun. Those eyes were captivating and were what kept Lucifer's attention the most.

After the woman was done her bath, she would meander about the garden tending to the animals, both big and small. No creature was frightened of her, nor she of them. She would help bear cubs get honey from a tree, but then bring flowers to the bees. She would run wild with the wolves and wrestle their pups, but also save tiny bunnies from being teased by those same pups. She would help snails get to hard-to-reach places and help birds fix their feathers. All life was precious to her, and she loved taking care of the animals. Her favorite thing to do was to help mothers deliver their babies and get them to nurse for the first time. Nothing brought more joy to her than seeing that.

Lucifer could tell that the woman longed to be a mother. Thus far, it had been his greatest challenge. No matter what he had tried to do, he could not get them to procreate. The two had mated several times but a child had yet to take. Could one of them be flawed? He would often think to himself, but then immediately retract the thought, knowing that God had made them exactly how he intended. But what more was he to do? He could tell that there was a hole in her heart that saddened her. He too, felt empty at times. Even though he was surrounded by life and beauty, and he was kept busy with his tasks, Lucifer was alone. He had not seen his father since the day God had brought mankind to the garden. He had not seen his siblings in an even longer time. Not since they all were sent away to create their gardens a millennium ago.

He recalled the early days when he and his siblings would rest within their sanctuary, overlooking the current universe at that time. Raphael would be somewhere behind the group doing whatever exercise pleased him. Gabriel would be slouched against the nearest thing that would hold him upright, trying to catch a few minutes of sleep. Uriel would be sitting above her two older brothers, listening in as Lucifer passed his knowledge onto his most beloved brother, Michael.

The five of them shared a bond like no other. Despite their differences, they were always united, and he missed them dearly.

Back in the Garden, Lucifer sat perched on top of a high tree under the cover of night. He craved communication the same way the woman longed for a child. But he could not reveal himself; that was his father's command.

However, the loneliness weighed on him. Lucifer found himself becoming depressed, which was starting to limit him in fulfilling his tasks.

So, he convinced himself that he would approach the woman in his serpent form, pretending to be injured. The woman would take him into her care, allowing Lucifer to get close to the man and woman. He would have his connection and be able to figure out why a child has not yet been conceived.

The angel smiled to himself at the thought of this new plan. He felt excited to finally be up close to the humans and to be a part of their lives since he had remained hidden and undetected for so long. He would finally be able to solve the last piece of the puzzle to bring about God's full plan for mankind.

Lucifer transformed back into the silver snake and curled up on a branch that overhung the pond. As he began to doze off, he ended his day with the thought that tomorrow he would finally be able to step out of the shadows.

Chapter
3

Into the Light.

Asudden sound of water splashing awakened Lucifer. The sun was shining directly on him, and as he blinked his eyes into focus, he could see ripples traveling across the pond's surface. He lifted his head slightly to get a better view of what could have caused the ripples, but saw nothing. The sun's reflection on the water made it difficult to see at this angle, but his primary concern was that he could also sense nothing. This made him go into a state of alert. He poised his body into a striking position and readied himself to transform if necessary. He stared intensely at the pond, searching for anything out of the ordinary.

The pond swelled as if breathing. Then the surface split, and a raven-haired woman burst through, sending an arc of water cascading over Lucifer.

This truly startled the serpent and caused him to fall from his branch into the water. He popped his head out of the water and began swimming to the edge. "Well, this is new." He thought to himself, embarrassed as he continued to swim.

Then he felt a hand under his belly and a soft, comforting voice say, "Here, let me help you." Lucifer's head quickly turned around and locked eyes with the woman. For the first time in his existence,

Lucifer went rigid. Cold water swirled around him, yet a warmth pulsed through his coils, rising to his chest until he could hardly breathe. A rush of thoughts and emotions ran through his mind that he had never felt before, and caused his body to go limp.

"What is happening to me?" He thought to himself.

The woman, sensing that something was amiss, put Lucifer around her neck and finished swimming to the edge of the pond.

As she rose out of the water, she cupped his head in her right hand and held the base of his body in her left. Once on land, she lifted his head and turned him so that their eyes could meet once more. "Hello friend, I haven't seen you here before." She said with a welcoming smile.

Lucifer just stared back at her, still in a state of confusion.

"You poor thing." The woman continued. "That must have been frightening for you. I'm going to place you here in the sun to warm up, but I will be back to check on you later." She then gently pulled Lucifer off her body, kneeled, and placed him in a coil on the ground. The whole time, they never broke eye contact. She held his head in the palm of her hand and slowly let it slip off her fingers. They held each other's gaze, her eyes bright with curiosity and wonder. In his mind, feelings swirled like storm clouds, strange and unnamable currents he had never known before. He couldn't put it into words because he had never felt this before. He just stared at the woman smiling at him. The woman caressed his head one more time before she stood up and walked away.

Lucifer continued to stare at her until she faded from sight and still stared at the spot where she did. Finally, he broke his own silence. "What have I done?" he asked himself. "No, no, no, this is not how it was supposed to happen. Yes, it didn't go as planned, but the scenario would have still worked. But... when she touched me, I couldn't move. And when our eyes met, something came over me. What was that?"

He began to fear that his plan was all for naught. He feared that this was what his father had meant by telling him to never interfere. He got angry with himself and decided that he would stay away from the woman and continue to only do what he was directed to do. He started to slither away, but only got a few feet before stopping. With every coil he dragged away from the spot, a hollow ache opened inside him, like roots tearing free from soil. However, his mind was made up, and he began slithering away once more.

He climbed up a tall tree that overlooked the spot where the woman had set him down. He was far enough away and hidden behind a group of leaves where he would be able to see her, but she would not be able to see him.

A few hours passed before the woman would be seen again. He watched her walk up the path toward the spot where she had left him. The sun illuminated her body as it moved rhythmically to the recoil of each step. Again, Lucifer felt that strange sensation beginning to rise within him. The woman got a few feet from her destination and stopped once she saw that the blue-eyed silver serpent was no longer there. She began to search for him in the surrounding areas. As she was searching, all Lucifer wanted to do was call out to her, but forced himself not to.

After a few minutes of searching, the woman sat back on her feet, her hands on her hips, eyes scanning the undergrowth. A sigh escaped her lips, and a flicker of disappointment softened her face. Lucifer saw this. "Did she feel as I did?" he asked himself. "No, that would be impossible. I was nothing more than a snake to her. She treated me like she does all the other animals in the land. Stop being a fool."

But the woman stayed where she was. Her eyes were searching for any sign of him. The woman then noticed the path that he had made while he slithered away. She stood up and started to follow the trail. Lucifer watched as she got closer and closer to the tree he was in. He slowly uncoiled his body and stretched it to perfectly rest on top of the branch he was on, so that from the ground, you would not be able to see him.

He could no longer see her, but he could hear her walking around the tree. "Are you up there?" She called out. Again, Lucifer wanted to acknowledge her but held his tongue. The woman circled the tree several times but eventually stopped and started to walk away. Lucifer turned his head so that he could see her. The woman stopped walking and looked over her shoulder, but stared at the ground. "I know you're up there somewhere. I am sorry that I scared you earlier. I hope to see you again." Then she turned her head and began walking back down the path.

Lucifer was heartbroken. He held himself still, every instinct screaming to dive after her. Yet reason chained him to the branch, muscles tight as bowstrings.

When night fell, he slid down the tree and headed to where the man and woman slept. Upon arriving there, he saw that the man was fast asleep, but the woman was sitting up, staring at the night sky. Her arms were wrapped under her legs, and her hair was swaying gently in the breeze. Even from where Lucifer was sitting, he could see the moon reflecting off her eyes. She was incredibly beautiful.

He watched her for a moment before deciding to turn around. But then he heard the woman sniffle, and he turned back to see what was happening. The woman wasn't staring into the sky; she was looking at a bird nest where a mother and father bird were protecting it.

It was at that moment that Lucifer knew that he was right in his thinking. He had to get close to figure out why the woman could not become a mother. His father had entrusted him to make sure that the man and woman populated the Garden. So, he decided to put everything else to the side and focus on his mission.

He slithered up to the woman, who was still looking at the nest, and stopped at her side to not startle her. He then gently and softly bumped her with his nose, but the woman did not move. He tried again, a little harder this time, which caused the woman to simply brush her leg. Finally, Lucifer raised his body up and set his head on the woman's knee. This made the woman flinch and look down, but once she saw it was him, her tears faded, and a smile formed. "Hello, my friend!" she said in a hushed but excited voice.

Lucifer snaked his way around her leg, then around her waist and torso before coming to rest on her shoulders. Once again, they made eye contact. 'Don't ever leave me,' she murmured, resting her forehead to his. Lucifer's breath caught. 'Never,' he whispered, the word a vow he intended to keep, not aware of its cost.

Chapter
4

The Original Sin

In the coming days and weeks, the woman grew quite fond of her new pet snake. It was highly intelligent, able to help her with tasks, and became an extension of herself. It would sit on her shoulders and go swimming with her. They would take care of the other animals together. It would even help the man in the garden by burrowing trenches to plant seeds or digging up planted vegetables. The man and woman cherished the serpent as it did them.

For Lucifer, he rather enjoyed the company of the man and woman. He had spent so much time observing them from afar that he felt thrilled to be in their presence. Mainly because he was no longer alone. But he did not let his excitement overshadow his goal. The man and woman had mated twice in his time with them, and he still could not sense a new life. This puzzled him. They are mating the proper way, and everything appeared to be functioning the way it was intended to, but why could a child not be conceived?

Lucifer pondered and sought out many solutions. He watched other species mate and what they did before mating. What foods they ate, how much water they drank, and the way they acted before mating. He was able to get the man and woman to eat the same foods and drink the same water, and they were able to do the movements on their own, yet they still could not conceive. This baffled Lucifer.

The man seemed content with his lifestyle. Lucifer could tell that he cared for the woman and could see her concerns, but what was he to do? The garden still needed tending, so each day the man continued to carry on as he always did.

However, the woman began to struggle. She would still get up in the morning, but would not take her daily swim. She would still care for the animals, but not with a smile on her face as she normally would. At night, she would hold onto Lucifer as if he were her child, cradling him in her arms. Her warm, soft skin felt good on his cool scales. Lucifer knew that he had to take a risk, for he could sense a darkness taking hold of the woman. The same mental darkness that caused him to come to her aid to begin with.

Later that night, while the man and woman were fast asleep, Lucifer slithered away and transformed into his angelic state. With a wave of his hand, he hushed the land. By doing this, Lucifer put all living organisms in a comatose state so that he could move freely without being caught as an angel.

He walked over to the man and woman and laid them on their backs. Using his divine sight, he investigated their bodies. He could see their veins, nerves, and muscles as well as their bones and organs. He watched as their blood pumped into their hearts and dispersed throughout their bodies. He stood there for hours comparing the two, his head swaying back and forth as he investigated for flaws. "Flaws," he said to himself. "Father doesn't make flaws." But as he said this, he notices something within the man's genitalia. Lucifer cannot see the movement in the man's groin as he has seen in the other male animals. He moves closer to get a better look, and as he does, he realizes the man is infertile.

Lucifer sits down, puzzled by his findings. "Why would Father make this man imperfect? If the goal was to have them mate and multiply, why then would the man not be able to do so?" He lays back and looks to the sky. His mind races, searching for a solution or an answer to this question.

30

Before he realizes it, the first signs of morning begin to appear and cause him to snap out of his thoughts. He quickly unhushes the land and disappears into the brush, transforms back into the serpent and climbs into the apple tree next to the pond.

He sits there, motionless, staring into the water. "Never have I questioned my father's actions before. Doing so goes against everything that I know, yet here I sit doing it." A million thoughts are running through his head, then suddenly.

"There you are!" the woman exclaims, breaking his thoughts.

He turns to look at her as she is walking up to him. Once again, their eyes meet. Lucifer is captivated by her. With all the beauty of the garden, it fails in comparison to her. She truly is perfect. The woman reaches out and scratches under his chin. "Swim with me," she says.

Lucifer uncoils from the tree and wraps himself around her body. Together, they dive into the crystal waters to the bottom, where they spiral with one another, maintaining eye contact the whole time, only surfacing so that the woman can breathe.

They swim for hours together before the woman gets out and lays on the shoreline, bathing in the warm sunlight. Lucifer crawls back into the apple tree and looks down at the woman. He admires the form of her body. Her soft chest fades into her toned stomach. Her hips slightly bulge at her sides, forming into her shapely legs down to her perfect feet. She is a sight that he could never grow tired of looking at.

The two sit in silence for a bit, listening to the sounds of the garden. But the silence is broken by a soft grumble of hunger from the woman. Lucifer does a quick flick of his tail and knocks an apple off the tree, making it land perfectly in the woman's hand. She opens her eyes and smiles up at him. "Thank you, my friend," she says warmly as she takes a bite.

"Lucifer."

A voice says to her within her own head. The woman shoots upright and looks around, startled and confused.

"My name is Lucifer."

This time, the voice is not in her head. She looks at the apple tree to see the silver serpent staring directly at her.

"Lucifer is the name that my father gave me. The one whom you call God."

The woman is frozen in fear. Nothing has ever talked to her before, aside from the man and God. Lucifer, seeing that the woman is about to run away, quickly tries to calm her down.

"I am sorry that I have deceived you for so long. I was told that I could not divulge my true nature to you. Please, do not be frightened. If I wanted to hurt you, I would have done so already."

Slowly, the woman starts to relax.

"I promise I will tell you everything come nightfall, and the man is asleep. Until then, we must act in a manner that will not attract attention. Do you trust me?" Lucifer asks gently.

The woman's eyes move back and forth as she tries to comprehend what is taking place. She is fearful and uncertain, yet still, she feels a calmness within her heart. "For reasons unknown to me... I do." She replies.

The woman allows Lucifer to climb onto her. They stare at each other as he does so.

"I know what I ask of you is difficult, and I am sorry that I must ask you to deceive the man. Can you give me tonight to explain?"

The woman looks off in deep thought. Without a word, she wraps him over her shoulders, and together they walk down the path. Once they return home, she does her best to act natural until the man falls asleep.

She lays next to him for a while to ensure that he is in a deep sleep, then turns over to look at Lucifer, who isn't there?

She sits up, "Lucifer?" she whispers. No response. She gets up and starts to search for him, but cannot find him. "The tree!" she says to herself. She takes one last look at the man to make sure that he is still asleep, then heads off to the pond.

Once she arrives at the pond, she again calls out for Lucifer.

"I am here," his voice comes from within again.

"Where?" she asks.

A calm stillness moves past her as though everything has fallen asleep.

"Before I show myself to you, I must ask you once more. Do you trust me?"

The woman hesitates again before replying. "Yes, I do."

A golden aurora begins to shine from deep in the center of the pond. Slowly, it rises, and the woman is able to make out the shape of a shadowy figure within the glow. At first, the figure is blurry, but then, as it gets closer, it starts to look like a creature with horns protruding from his head. But the light is so bright that it makes it hard to see clearly. As the figure breaches the surface of the water, she realizes that they are not horns, but wings folded behind its back. The figure rises completely out of the water and spreads his wings to the fullest.

Before her is an angel of the Lord. His head is tilted to the sky with his eyes closed, water dripping from his hair. His arms are out towards the ground with welcoming hands. His right leg, bent at the knee, is slightly higher than his left. As the light begins to dull, the angel lowers himself to the water's surface, where his foot stands on it as though it were solid.

Finally, the angel comes to rest on the water. He folds his hands inside the sleeves of his robe, looks in the direction of the woman, and opens his eyes.

As soon as she sees his eyes, she knows that it is indeed Lucifer. The color of his eyes is identical to that of the serpent that she has stared into for the last few months.

"Are you afraid of me?" Lucifer asks her. She shakes her head. "Good." He says, smiling. "I am Lucifer, the first son of God. I am the first angel ever to be created, and I made this garden that we stand in now." He says while looking around.

The woman looks around with him, in awe of what she is seeing and hearing.

Lucifer continues, "My father created you and the man and set me, along with my siblings, on a task to create a home for you to live in. The other gardens were flawed in some manner or another, so my father chose my garden to be your home. I was tasked to watch over you both and ensure that you fulfilled the plan that my father has set in place for you."

The woman looks back at Lucifer.

"But you are not fulfilled, are you?" He asks her. "You long to be a mother. A wish the man cannot grant you."

The woman lowers her head as tears begin to form. Suddenly, she feels a hand lift her chin. She looks up to see Lucifer now standing directly in front of her. He is astonishingly handsome. Far more than the man. His silk white hair blowing gently. A soft smile rests on his face. And his eyes. His eyes are so mesmerizing that she feels weak in the knees. "This is the snake that I have cared for so dearly? The snake who is an angel?" She confusingly asks herself. "But he feels so warm and comforting. I do not feel this way towards the man. What is this feeling?"

In truth, she has always felt it. She has felt this way since the day their eyes first met in the pond. In that moment, the two had fallen in love. And now here he is, in his true form, and he is magnificent. She just stares into his eyes as he bends down so that his forehead can meet hers.

"The man cannot give you what you wish," he speaks gently to her. "But I can."

And with that, the two embrace in a kiss, then another and another. The woman grabs the back of Lucifer's head and pulls him in tight. He grabs her legs and pulls her up to him as he straightens back up. Lucifer then spreads his wings and gently floats down until the woman lands softly on her back. He stops kissing the woman and stares into her eyes, and she returns his gaze. She then reaches up and pulls him back to her, and while she is bringing him closer, he enters her.

She lets out a soft, pleasured moan as she feels him fill her from within. Her deep panting breaths filling his ear with each thrust. She claws at the back of his head, pulling it deep into her neck as he presses her back against the grass.

A stillness falls across the land. The flowers next to them begin to wilt ever so slightly. The stream slows, and the water in the pond clouds a little. The animals stir in their sleep, and their fur starts to shed for the first time. An apple falls off the tree, and the night gets a little darker.

As the human and the angel conceive life... the garden begins to lose it.

The act of the Original Sin has been committed.

Chapter

5

The Woman's Name

Life in the garden had changed. Not drastically, but as time went on, the garden dulled. The colors were not as vibrant, the fruit was not as sweet, and the water was not as pure as it once was. All subtle, trivial things that the man and woman barely took notice of. But Lucifer noticed it all.

He spent his days slithering all over the garden, trying to breathe his essence into it all. It would work for a brief period of time, but as soon as he stopped, it would fade again. Try as he might, he could not return the garden to its original state. The garden was beginning to die.

Death was new to Lucifer. At the time, Lucifer did not even know what death was, for it had never existed to him before now. But he knew something was wrong.

He did not let his concerns show to the woman. When he wasn't trying to fix the garden, he spent time with her and the man as he did before. Although when it was just Lucifer and the woman, they would talk to each other. At night, he would hush the man so that the woman and he could hold and love one another.

He would look into her belly and watch his children grow. They were just two tiny black dots at first, but over the coming weeks, he would see little limbs growing and small eyes forming. He would describe what he was seeing in detail to the woman, and she would smile ear to ear. She was thrilled and loved the fact that she was going to have two children, but even more so, she was in love with Lucifer.

He was everything that the man wasn't. He was caring and actually listened to her thoughts and wonders. He was patient and kind in teaching her new things about the world. He would even take her on trips to the areas beyond her home. She loved the way he smelled when he held her. His skin was soaked in the fragrance of the flowers that he tended to. His strong hands were gentle when they were on her, bringing her a sense of security.

She often found herself thinking about what their children would look like. Would they take after her or their father? Would they have his wings? But more importantly, she thought about how Lucifer would look while caring for them. The thought of him cradling two infants in his big, strong arms made her cheeks blush and elevated her heart rate.

Soon, the woman began to show, and the man started to notice. Lucifer had to sit there and watch as the man showed excitement and kissed the woman he loved. He watched the man care for her freely and unrestricted, not bound by any limitations. He knew that it needed to be this way, but Lucifer soon started to resent the man.

One day, as they were walking through the garden, Lucifer sat silently on her shoulders in his serpent form.

After a while, the woman broke the silence. "You're not very talkative today. What's wrong?"

Lucifer waited for a moment before responding. "It bothers me when I see you and the man being affectionate towards one another. The man is not deserving of you."

The woman stops walking and looks at him. "You said that we were to keep this a secret. That we could not let the man know of your true existence and that we were to continue to live as we did before that night so that nothing would seem out of place." She responded firmly.

Lucifer turns his head. He knew she was right, but it didn't rid him of his troubles.

"Look at me." The woman commanded softly. Again, he paused before reacting. When he did look back at her, she said, "I love you. I love the two babies growing inside of me. I love us." Her eyes begin to water. "The man is nothing more to me now than a friend to care for. You are my one love," she says as she holds the side of Lucifer's face.

Lucifer looks down. "I love you all as well."

"Then why do you question me?" she asks as she pulls his gaze back to her.

Lucifer pulls away again. "I don't know. All of this is new to me. I have to watch the man touching all over the woman that I love. The woman that is bearing my children. Things are changing in the garden. It's like life is being drained out of everything, and I cannot figure out why."

The woman puts her finger over his lips to silence him as she uses her other hand to hold her stomach. "Maybe it's because the garden is helping to grow the seeds you have planted."

It takes a moment for the realization of what the woman had just said to fully enter Lucifer's mind. But then his eyes widen and fill with delight. "That's it!" he excitedly says to himself. He turns and looks at the woman. "You're absolutely right!" he exclaims to her and begins to ramble on.

"That makes absolute sense. Life can only be created by life. I had the garden fully sustained with what was in it. It would always have what it needed as long as the cycle continued uninterrupted," he said hurriedly. "But we added to it, we disrupted the cycle, so now the garden must disperse its energy accordingly!"

Lucifer wrapped his body around the woman and pressed his head against hers. "Thank you," he whispers to her.

She kisses his nose and says, "We must do whatever it takes to ensure that our children have the best possible life. If that means you have to tend to the garden more and I need to continue lying with the man, then so be it. Our love is strong, and our love for our children is even stronger. We can weather anything that life throws at us."

"I agree," Lucifer responds. "However, I cannot watch you be with the man as I have been."

"You need not," she responds understandingly. "We will meet at the apple tree each night. You can hush the man, and we can be together. Just the four of us."

Lucifer nods his head in agreement. The woman uncoils him and places him on a nearby tree branch at eye level, her eyes full of admiration. "I will see you tonight, my love," she says as she kisses his head before walking away.

"Wait!" Lucifer shouts to her. She quickly turns around to face him. "You know my name, but I have no name to call you."

"I do not have a name," she responds.

"I know." Lucifer replies, "So let's give you one," he says, smiling.

He slithers over and begins to circle around her slowly, deep in thought as he examines her. She was incredibly beautiful. Lucifer couldn't find a flaw in her. He watched the golden flecks in her eyes glimmer as strands of black hair danced across her face. This sight made him want to pause time there for an eternity.

In truth, giving her a name had never crossed his mind. But he viewed her as everything he was not. She fulfilled him. Completed him. And he, her. They had become one with each other. If he were a shining star, then she would be the moon. If he belonged to the day, then she would belong to the night. And she was his love.

He stops circling her and slowly blinks, pleased with himself for the name he has chosen. He stretches up to meet her eye-to-eye.

"Lilith."

He says confidently.

"Your name is Lilith."

The woman leans in and presses their heads together, smiling as she does so. "Lilith," she whispers in approval.

Lilith pulls her head back and smiles at Lucifer. "Tonight, my love." She says before turning and walking away with a little bounce in her step, leaving Lucifer to remain smiling as he watches her fade into the brush.

Chapter 6

The Promise

Months go by as Lucifer and Lilith carry on in their agreed-upon way. During the day, she spends time with the man, who has been helping her with her tasks as well as his own. Life is different for them from what it was before, but the man doesn't mind. His days may be longer, but he cares for the woman and knows that he is needed.

Lilith does as much as she can in the garden, but needs to stop and take breaks periodically. She sits on the pond's edge and dips her toes into the water. She has noticed that it is much colder than it was before. She wraps her arms around her belly and talks and sings to her children as she slowly swirls her feet around.

Lucifer has told her that she will be giving birth soon. He checks the children every night and tells them what he sees. She already loves them with every fiber of her being and can't wait to see them. But she has to keep reminding herself to be patient. Lucifer says that they will come when the three of them are ready. So, she rests while she can in her spot by the pond, taking in the beauty of the garden. It has definitely changed; she can see it now.

Lucifer spends his time tending the garden. Time flows differently for him when he is away from Lilith and the man, and he is glad that it does. It takes a long time and a lot of energy to keep the garden sustained. He knows that eventually he will need to expand it to the rest of the lands, but that will have to wait until the children are born. He can barely keep up with what he has now.

He works hard to make sure that all life in the garden has what it needs to continue living, but in doing so, it weakens him. Sometimes he questions if there is more of him in the garden than what is in his own body.

But every night, he regains some of his strength. Holding onto Lilith and looking at his children within her brings much joy and motivation to him. He looks forward to his time with Lilith. He loves her and does everything he does so that she can be happy. So, he presses on, knowing that soon he will be able to watch her become a mother and thrilled by the thought of seeing her holding their children.

Lucifer takes a break and looks up to the sky. It is a beautiful night sky with not a cloud in sight. Purples and blues provide a backdrop for the millions of light orbs that blanket the heavens.

Suddenly, reality sets in. "It's nighttime!" he exclaims as he turns and rushes to the pond.

As he nears the pond, he can hear Lilith talking. He is about to call out to her, but he hears the man's voice and slows his slither. He creeps his way closer and comes to rest under a bush, allowing him to be hidden as he watches.

Lilith is sitting under the apple tree, as she normally does, looking up at the man. "Why are you out here?" he asks her. "I woke up and couldn't find you. I was so worried that something had happened."

"I'm sorry, my dear," Lilith replies. "I have trouble sleeping at night, so sometimes I come here to relax myself."

The man is confused but decides not to ask any more questions. Instead, he says, "Well, if this is where you are comfortable, then I will stay here with you," and lays down next to her.

Lilith looks and smiles at him, then turns her focus back to the surrounding area, searching for any sign of Lucifer.

Across the pond, she sees two small eyes reflected by the moonlight. "Is that you?" She whispers in her mind.

"Yes," Lucifer replies.

"Where have you been?! Look at what has happened in your absence," she says sternly.

"I am sorry, my love. I was tending to the garden, and time had gotten away from me." Lucifer responds.

"The garden has you during the day. At night, we are your garden," she says as she places a hand on her stomach. "Fix this now."

Lucifer nods to her and slithers away. He cannot transform back into an angel that close to the man, or he would notice him. When he is a safe distance away, he transforms and hushes the land before returning to Lilith. "We are alone now," he says to her.

Lilith does not meet his eyes. He can see by the look on her face that she is not happy with the current situation. So, he bends down, picks the man up, and carries him away and out of sight. Upon his return, he sees that Lilith has now laid on her side, facing away from him. He lets out a small sigh before walking up and laying down next to her. "I am sorry," he says as he puts his arm around her and kisses the back of her head.

Lilith rolls over to face him with tears in her eyes. "You have become distant these past few weeks. Each day you get here later and later, and now today, almost too late," she says in a crackled voice. "I need you here with me. With us," she says as the tears trickle down her cheeks.

Lucifer presses his forehead against hers. "I will be, I promise. I am here with you and will be forever. I swear it."

Hearing this makes Lilith smile, and the two embrace in a loving kiss.

A swift kick in the stomach breaks Lucifer from his love's embrace. He chuckles as he places his hand on Lilith's stomach. "I will always be there for you two as well, my sons.

Lilith's eyes widened in excitement. "Sons?!" she shouts.

This is the first time that Lucifer has divulged what gender their children are. "I was trying to keep it a surprise, but tonight felt like the right time to tell you," he says, smiling.

Again, Lilith's eyes fill with tears. Although they are of joy this time. "Tell me about them," she asks gleefully.

Lucifer looks into her belly to see his sons. Normally, he sees them moving around and grabbing aimlessly at one another. But not this time. This time, as he fixes his gaze on them, he pauses and lets out a small gasp. "What is it?" Lilith asks with concern in her voice.

Lucifer hesitated, his voice breaking. "They are… They… They are looking at me." The words felt heavy in his mouth, as though the children's stares carried a weight he could not explain.

Chapter

7

The Darkness

The next morning, as Lucifer is going about his business in the garden, he cannot stop thinking about the children being able to see him. It wasn't a mere coincidence; he tried testing it. No matter where he moved, they turned and watched him. He did it for so long that Lilith had to ask him to stop because she was getting nauseous from the children moving around so much. He went and got the sleeping man and laid him down next to Lilith as he was before. Then Lucifer turned into his serpent form and went back to tending the garden.

By mid-morning, he tended a rose bush, but then the garden fell silent. The birds ceased their songs, the animals stilled, and even the breeze seemed to retreat, leaving a silence so complete it pressed against his ears. The birds had stopped singing, and the animals had stopped chattering. Even the gentle breeze seemed to have slowed down next to nothing at all. This caused Lucifer to come to full alert. He slithered into an open area and listened to the land, trying to hear or sense anything that could be amiss. Every muscle in his body was tense and ready to strike or evade if necessary.

Then he felt it. Cold, suffocating, familiar. Darkness had come for the garden, and Lucifer's heart clenched at the memory of battles long past.

But how? He and his father, along with his siblings, had defeated the Darkness and pushed it back long ago.

The Darkness is a plague that ravages like a storm through time and space. It is everything and nothing at the same time. Just a vast void that overcomes everything in its path and drains the life of whatever it touches.

For ages uncounted, God waged war against the Darkness alone. At last, even His strength faltered, and so He shaped a companion from pure light. Thus was born Lucifer, the first angel. Prior to the birth of the other four angels, God and Lucifer created orbs of energy and scattered them throughout the infinite void of the Darkness. This provided beacons of light all over, which in turn, provided safe havens for God and Lucifer. They called them stars, brilliant beacons scattered across the endless void. Each flame burned as a promise that the Darkness would not consume all.

Their energies were so powerful that they obliterated the Darkness, but only within a certain area. This caused a need for more and more stars to be made, and the task was far too large for only God and Lucifer. So, that is when God created the other angels to help.

Michael, Raphael, Uriel, and Gabriel, along with Lucifer, made up the five archangels of God. Together, they created so many stars that the Darkness was able to be held at bay. However, God knew that even the stars would eventually fail, and the Darkness would return. He sought a greater power, not one to be mastered, but one that could be coaxed into balance, a raw force that would defy both Light and Darkness.

God began working on it and set forth his angels to create worlds that would allow this new power to roam freely. Tirelessly, he worked in solitude to create this new power and succeeded. In his hand, he held a tiny white ball full of the strongest energy possible. It was difficult for even him to hold, but he had planned for this.

Prior to its creation, God knew that the power would require a vessel to be housed in. So, he created the man. The man was made in his image so that the power would recognize and not destroy its host.

But God also knew that only one of these orbs would not be enough, which led him to create a woman. Since the woman would not be created in God's image, he used a piece from the man to create her so that she too, could hold the energy within her.

God's plan was to place an orb in both the man and the woman, place them in the right garden that one of his children made, and have them reproduce to create more of this energy. That would be the only way to defeat the Darkness, with more light. He called this energy a soul, and he made it so that it could never be destroyed.

Once a soul was placed in the man and woman, it would give them life. It would also give them the ability to move and think freely, not bound or tethered to anything. Freewill. The man and woman would procreate, which would take a small amount of energy from each of their souls and make a new soul. This new soul would then create a body for itself using parts from its mother and father.

This would be how more light would be created. A soul would stay with its host forever, providing it with life while also growing stronger until it reached its full potential and turned its host into a divine deity. At which point, God would turn it into a star. Then that star would be so bright and powerful that not only would it keep the Darkness at bay, but it would also provide life to other surrounding gardens, allowing more souls to grow. Thus, creating an eternal and self-sustaining life cycle.

God's plan was to create an infinite amount of light so that the Darkness would be eliminated. And it would have worked had it not been interfered with. He knew that his plan was extremely volatile. One deviation from it and the whole thing would collapse. This is why he picked Lucifer and his garden to house the man and woman. Lucifer was the most devoted to fighting against Darkness. He was the only angel who had seen firsthand what its full power was.

But something had happened during Lucifer's creation that God could not avoid. God had created Lucifer while the Darkness surrounded him. Even though Lucifer was created by God, he was made within the dark. And because of this, Lucifer was indeed born from both the light and the dark. And since the Darkness dwelled within Lucifer, it would always be able to find him and corrupt him as it saw fit.

Which brings us back to the garden where Lucifer sits, frozen in fear. "This is not possible," he says to himself aloud. Suddenly, a shriek of pain comes screeching across the land. "Lilith!" Lucifer shouts. Quickly, he transforms into his angel form and races off to find her.

Chapter 8

The Nephilim

The sky has turned grey, and the wind has begun to howl by the time Lucifer is able to track down Lilith, who is at her favorite spot by the pond. He is high in the air, watching as Lilith is seated in a birthing position. The man is sitting behind her, holding her head and stroking her hair in a comforting manner. Lilith lets out another shrill scream of pain. Her body is covered in sweat, and she is clutching the man's hand as she cries.

Lucifer is hesitant about what to do. He knows that he will be of no use as a serpent, but also knows that he cannot show himself to the man.

Another scream pierces his ears as Lilith throws her head back and the two make eye contact. "I NEED YOU!" she cries.

That is all it took. Lucifer swoops down, and the man sees him for the first time. Startled by Lucifer's sudden appearance, the man lets go of Lilith and scampers back a few feet as Lucifer lands where he just had been.

The man watches as Lucifer comforts the woman, kisses her head, and says, "I am here, my love." This thoroughly confuses the man. What is this thing with a similar body to him but with the wings of a bird? Why does it glow? Why is the woman so comfortable with it? And why did it call her its love?

So many emotions are filling his head. He is confused, scared, worried, and feeling helpless. Then a deep, calming voice breaks his thoughts. "Whatever it is that you are feeling right now, I need you to put it aside and come help."

The man looks up to see the winged being staring at him. His eyes widen as he recognizes those eyes. "The snake?!" He exclaims.

"I will explain everything later," the creature says. "But for now, we need to help her give birth."

The man is shaking but nods his head and crawls back over.

Lucifer slides out from under Lilith and allows the man to take his place. He then moves to Lilith's lower body and peers into her stomach. The children have become wedged and unable to move. One of them is looking at Lucifer in fear and confusion. Lucifer looks up at Lilith and the man and says calmly, "They are stuck. I need to reach into you and separate them, or they will not make it."

Lilith looks down at him. "Do whatever you need to do," she says nervously yet confidently.

Lucifer nods and looks at the man. "Hold her tight, this is going to hurt her." The man secures Lilith by her arms as Lucifer reaches inside her. Lilith screams as her body naturally tries to escape the pain. "Hold her down," Lucifer says calmly at the man, keeping his composure. The man quickly puts all his strength into holding onto Lilith as Lucifer reaches farther inside.

He is still looking within her and making eye contact with the one child. "It will be ok," he says to it as he gently pushes the other child back into Lilith's stomach. As he pulls his hand out, he looks up to Lilith and tells her to take a deep breath and push. As she does this, the first child slides out of her and into Lucifer's hands. He looks down at his son as it looks up at him. Then the newborn lets out a long wail, and Lucifer quickly places it on Lilith's chest. The child immediately goes quiet within the comfort of its mother's arms, and Lilith begins to weep with joy at the sight of her child.

Lucifer then peers inside Lilith again to see if the other child is ready to come out. However, the child has not moved since Lucifer moved it out of the way. A sense of panic sets in, and Lucifer knows that he must get the child out as quickly as possible. He looks at Lilith and the man and says, "I need to open you up to get this one out."

Lilith's eyes widen as she can sense the concern in Lucifer's voice. "What's wrong?!" she asks in fear.

Lucifer does not respond. He looks at the man, and the two acknowledge what is about to happen without speaking a word. The man takes the child out of Lilith's reluctant arms and places it down gently out of harm's way. He then restrains a frantic Lilith and holds her with all his might. Lilith is in full panic mode. "What's wrong?! What are you doing?!" She screams

Lucifer looks Lilith in the eyes. "I am sorry." He then focuses his energy on the tip of his forefinger and begins to cut Lilith's stomach open. Lilith screams in agony but remains still as Lucifer reaches inside her and pulls the child out. He quickly cauterizes her wound and then focuses his attention on the unmoving child. He stares at its lifeless body in his blood-soaked hands. He starts rubbing its chest and trying to breathe life into it, but has no success. "Come on, little one. Come on!" He pleads with tears in his eyes.

Lilith is on her knees in front of him now. She cups the child's head in her hands as Lucifer continues trying to bring the child to life. The man is seated with his back against the apple tree, cradling the other child in his arms and watching as the woman and this winged creature are trying to save the other child.

Minutes go by as Lucifer and Lilith fail to save the infant. Lilith is now clutching the child in her arms and crying a pain that only a mother of a lost child can feel. Lucifer remains on his knees, watching as the blood drops off his fingers and onto the ground. He is crying from his loss, which is another new feeling to him. He stretches his head back and looks up to the heavens while the tears stream down his face. "Father!" he cries out in anguish. "Help me!"

Almost instantly, the sounds of the day-to-day life in the garden falls silent as a low and deep thunder cracks loudly from somewhere in the distance and ripples across the land. Soon after, lightning begins to flash directly above them. The clouds start churning as more and more lightning flashes. The thunder becomes louder and more frequent until suddenly it stops, and one large lightning bolt shoots down, blinding Lucifer and the others.

Lucifer shields his eyes with his hands, but still needs to squint to regain his focus. Once he is able to clearly see again, he excitedly searches for his father. However, he does not see him anywhere nearby. He shifts his focus to the sky, and hovering high above them all is God. Lucifer smiles as he stands to his feet, but once he meets his father's gaze, he knows something is wrong.

God is hovering with his left arm across his torso, providing his right arm a resting place while it holds his chin. His right hand is gently caressing his beard as he takes in the sight below. He sees Lucifer looking up at him with a smile, but he does not return it. He notices that Lucifer is about to fly up to him, but he holds his hand out, motioning for Lucifer to stop.

There is a lot for God to take in. Things have changed since the last time he was here. The garden is no longer as vibrant as it once was. There is a chill in the air, and even the creatures act differently. He has seen this before. Long ago, in a time before this one. The Darkness has begun taking its hold on this place.

He scans the area looking for the source of it all, hoping that it is something that can be snuffed out quickly. But he cannot find any one thing that appears to be a significant source. That is, until he looks down at Lucifer again and sees the stillborn child in Lilith's arms and another in the man's.

"No..." God says to himself in fear as his eyes widen. He looks up into the heavens, "Come to me," he commands before turning back to the child and floating down.

God lands on the other side of the pond. This confuses Lucifer and causes him to ask, "Father? What is wrong?"

Lucifer can see that God is timid, as though he is afraid of coming close, but still, he pleads. "Father, I need your help." He bends down and takes the stillborn from Lilith. "This child has yet to take its first breath. It's been so long, Father, it needs your help." Again, Lucifer tries to walk towards God.

"You will not bring that thing another step closer to me, or I will strike you down," God says sternly to him. This causes Lucifer to freeze in shock and confusion. He turns back to look at Lilith, who is also scared and confused, but more thunder starts before they have time to ask any questions. Lucifer and Lilith look up to the sky, and within seconds, four bolts of lightning land around God. When the dust settles, all four of Lucifer's siblings are standing by God.

Gabriel is the farthest away and to the left of God. He is looking around as if he is trying to solve a puzzle. Gabriel stands about a half of a foot shorter than Lucifer. He is lean and athletically toned with a clean-shaven face. He, like all the other angels, shares the same platinum white hair and blue eyes. His eyes are a deeper shade of blue but just as piercing. His hair is straight and rests just below shoulder length on his tan skin. He is the more light-hearted of the siblings, but knows when to be serious. He is very nimble and light on his feet and can often be found training himself to fly faster.

Uriel is also behind God to the left. She is staring at the child that Lucifer is holding. Uriel is what you would picture when you close your eyes and think of a beautiful angelic woman. She is also athletically toned, much like that of an Olympic runner. Her hair is long and reaches her lower back. Her eyes are sharp and focused, yet hold compassion and care within them. She has pale skin and is the group's caregiver, making sure that everyone has what they need and that they take the time to rest. However, she is also a fierce warrior with the ability to teleport. Even though she is the smallest of the siblings, she is just as much of a threat as any of them. She wears a long robe like her brothers, but hers is more free-flowing, giving her better mobility.

Raphael is to God's right, and the same distance back as Uriel. He is also visibly angry and has his gaze fixated on the man and the living child. Raphael is monstrous in size, only falling just short of

God's height. He has a bronze skin tone and is built as though God had chiseled him from boulders. He is by far the strongest physically of the siblings. His hair is closely cropped, and he wears only the bottom half of his robe. His own personal aspirations have enabled him to replace Lucifer as the most devoted to the cause of fighting the Darkness, often allowing his drive to overshadow other things. He views those other things as distractions from the cause and is often alone, training for the next fight.

And then there is Michael, who is standing directly to God's right. He is the only sibling looking at Lucifer, confusion, and betrayal rest on his face. Michael has ebony skin and wears his white hair in locks that fall to the middle of his back. He has a close-cropped beard and a strong jawline. His eyes are identical to Lucifer's. He has a solidly built body and is more than capable of holding his own, even against Raphael. He is the most well-rounded angel, but his biggest strength is his mind. Michael is able to access situations and come up with multiple different outcomes, then acts on the best ones. He is a strategic thinker and very adept in battle, but will seek to avoid conflict if at all possible. He and Lucifer share the closest bond between all the siblings. He was the next to be created after Lucifer and has always looked to him for guidance. But now... now, he finds himself in a situation where not even he can tell what the outcome will be.

The four angels are loyal to their father and to the battle against the Darkness, up until this point. The six of them had all been on the same page. But things are different now as they await their father's command. Anticipation hangs in the air.

Lucifer, upon seeing his sibling's arrival, immediately knows something is wrong. He takes a few steps backward so that he doesn't break eye contact with anyone as he gives the lifeless child back to Lilith. "Go sit with the man." He tells her. She looks at him, desperately wanting him to look back at her, but she can tell by how his eyes are fixed that she should just do what she is told.

Lucifer shifts his eyes between all who are standing before him. "Have you not come to help me?" he asks, already knowing the answer.

God's eyes are fixed on the children as he responds. "Do you know what you have done? What they are?" he hisses.

"They are children," Lucifer says.

God looks Lucifer in the eyes, a growl in his voice. "They are Nephilim. Half breeds. Unholy creatures capable of mass destruction. Beings with all the power of angels but with the free will of man." He pauses as he looks back at the children. "Vessels of the Darkness..." Then back to Lucifer. "...and they must be destroyed."

The other four angels are shocked by what God has just said. They are now looking at the children as well as Lucifer in anticipation of what will happen next.

God starts walking towards Lilith and her children. Fear overcomes her, and she frantically looks back and forth between God and Lucifer.

Lucifer's mind is racing. Everything is playing out in slow motion in his head as he tries to figure out what to do. What is his father talking about? He speaks as though he has seen these children before. He hears Lilith crying out to him for help. Does he save her and the children? Doing so means going against God. Does he allow his father to destroy the children? Allowing that means taking away innocent lives. Lives that he has bonded with and grown to love. It would take away the one thing that makes Lilith whole, her motherhood. It would erase everything that he has worked for. All that he has done would be for naught.

He needs to decide quickly; God is getting closer. He closes his eyes for just a moment and blocks everything out. He takes a deep breath, and, in that instant, he is hit with a vision. A vision of a garden more beautiful than his own. An absolutely perfect Eden. And just as quickly as the vision came, it vanished. Leaving Lucifer his answer as to what to do.

The next few moments set forth events that are irreparable. Many things happen at once. But it is in the moment immediately after Lucifer's vision that the fall of all creation begins. For it is in that moment that Lucifer becomes the first...

Fallen Angel.

Chapter 10

In the Beginning:
Part i

Long before the time of this story, another came and passed. If you have chosen to follow a religion based on one and only one God, then you would be familiar with the knowledge that God has been, is, and forever will be. He has no birth date nor place of origin. He is everything and everywhere at the same time.

But what if I were to open your curiosity to another option? What if God was not always God? What if he was once a simple life form that became God out of necessity? A being that was chosen to transform into a powerful entity as a last-ditch effort to defeat an enemy that had overcome all other tactics.

I apologize for diverting us from our current story and promise to get back to it soon. But first, I need to tell you this, or you will not understand what is to come.

You see, in a far-off history, the universe was engulfed in light, and the Darkness did not exist. A civilization thrived that had no hunger, no disease, illness, or wars. Even death was all but extinct.

All of that had faded into a time that was forgotten. Or so most thought.

Within this utopia, celestial beings lived a life of wealth and knowledge. These beings were humanoid yet translucent. Their bodies looked like light was racing through their veins. Each had a star-like diamond in the middle of their foreheads that shone brightly, matching their white eyes. They had cosmic gases surrounding their bodies that looked like smoke wisping around them.

Everyone worked together to achieve a common goal: to continue the spread of life and light. It was this goal that drove the Celestials to seek and expand as much as possible.

During their explorations, they found other intelligent life forms throughout the universe. They would learn from these life forms and, in some cases, if deemed fit, they would co-exist with them in order to continue making all living beings the best that they could be.

Though it took millennia for the perfect utopia to exist, it was eventually done. This perfect utopia was given the name of Eden. And by the time it was completed, there were no distinct species to be found in all the known current universe.

Life had been so far perfected that only one species existed, and they called themselves Angels. A race that held within them traces of every DNA from all intelligent life forms from every corner of existence. These humanoid beings could fly without wings, breathe underwater without gills, or live in extreme conditions with no repercussions. They had golden skin and eyes that were able to change color and size depending on what they were using them for. Though they were a single species, they still each had their own physical characteristics that allowed them to be individualized, such as hair color and facial structure. They constructed self-sustaining cities and interstellar bridges that allowed transport between galaxies in a matter of hours. They were nearly flawless.

However, the angels did possess a single deformity. They were infertile and unable to reproduce naturally. In order for the species to flourish, DNA splicing had to be done between a male and female angel to create a child. This procedure took weeks to achieve, and only the highest-ranking angels were permitted to conduct this very tedious task. These angels were known as Weavers.

One of these angels was named Elohim. Elohim was young compared to the other Weavers but just as brilliant. His sharp mind, attention to detail, and ambition allowed him to climb the ranks and become one of the Elders within the ranks of the Weavers. The Elders were the ones who held councils to discuss possible ways to solve the issue of infertility. Even though Elohim was respected by his peers, they still viewed him as naive due to his short time within the ranks. But this did not stop Elohim from trying to make a difference. He studied hard and conducted experiments along with the other Weavers, trying to solve their puzzle.

Through his studies and the abundance of evidence from those before, Elohim decided to turn his focus to the cosmos in search of an answer. Even though the angels had searched through them thoroughly, the universe was forever growing, and new lifeforms were being discovered. However, none of the lifeforms that had been discovered recently met the conditions of acceptance within the realm of the angels. But Elohim was convinced that the answer lied somewhere out there.

His search went from days to weeks, to months, to years. Many of his peers thought his search was in vain and pleaded with him to shift his focus to another direction, but he refused. The angel race came from the cosmos, and Elohim felt, with every fiber of his being, that the solution to their problem was also somewhere out there.

Then one day, years later, he found it.

A pale blue dot light-years away. This planet was so small that he almost didn't see it, but it showed all the promises of having intelligent lifeforms dwelling on it. So, Elohim met with the Weaver Council and was given permission to search this faraway planet. He immediately gathered his equipment and began his journey.

Two days later, Elohim arrived at the uncharted planet. He circled around the stratosphere searching for signs of life, but he could not detect any from his current distance away. So, he decided to venture onto the planet's surface. He knew from his own studies and from the studies of others that caution was always best when navigating an unknown planet. For not every planet was welcoming.

As he descended, he was taken in awe of the planet's beauty. It was full of thick vegetation and clear blue waters. Large islands full of hills and valleys dotted the surface, surrounded by vast oceans. The air was clean and smelled like a forest after a spring rain. Elohim was excited. These were all the signs of a planet that produced intelligent life.

He decided to land on the largest island in his sight. It had high mountains and many waterfalls that gave life to rivers and streams. These waters held various aquatic lifeforms that had never been documented before. Elohim quickly began studying them. He took notes and drew pictures while giving them temporary names. He placed markers around so that he could later return with a full research team. These markers were small, transparent stickers that would mold into whatever surface they were placed on and would light up whenever an angel was near them.

He walked around for hours in a state of euphoria, taking in all the new discoveries. He found several new lifeforms, but none of which met the criteria that he was searching for, and it was beginning to become dark. He decided to go to the peak of the highest mountain to observe the island at night.

For a while, all Elohim was able to take in were the sounds of running water and strange noises that he assumed were the calls of the wildlife. But then, off in the distance, he saw a warm yellow glow. It was small, but unmistakable. "Fire!" he said to himself, and off he went to investigate.

Elohim proceeded with caution and landed a short distance away from the fire's location. Quietly, he crept through the brush until he was able to see the flames. He remained silent and observed from a safe location, hidden by the giant leaves of an alien plant. He could immediately tell that the fire was not made from natural causes. This fire had been erected by dry timbers that had been placed in a circle. A large flat rock lay next to it with fish from the river drying on top.

Elohim's heart began to race. These were the signs that he had been searching for these last few years. He eagerly wanted to get closer, but controlled his curiosity. He knew that he needed to wait to see what had started this fire.

As he peered into the flames, he began to notice the light of other fires scattered throughout the region. He had been waiting for some time to see if whatever made this fire would return, but it hadn't yet. He waited another few minutes, but still nothing.

Just as he was getting ready to go investigate another one of the fires, he saw it. Elohim's eyes widened in disbelief. It was hard for him to process what he was seeing, and his heart began to race.

The vegetation stirred, shadows shifting in the glow of the fire. From the brush emerged a figure...humanoid, carrying the resonance of an angel, yet primitive. This being was a female with an infant harnessed around her. She had dark hair and bronze skin. Her eyes were the colors of amber gemstones that seemed to glow from the light of the fire.

Elohim was paralyzed by the wave of emotions that he was having. He had hoped that he would find an answer, but he never imagined it to be this. And best of all, it had what appeared to be a very newly born child with it. He had to fight back the temptation of carting off the two back to the Weavers. He had to see if there were more like them. So, he placed another marker and then quietly slipped away before taking back to the sky.

Quickly, he flew to the next fire, then the next. Each fire had more and more of these humanoid beings. Males, females, and children. Elohim knew without a doubt that these beings were capable of reproducing naturally. He decided not to waste another minute and began his journey home.

In the Beginning: Part ii

Elohim returned to Eden as quickly as he could. Once there, he rushed to the Weavers Council and disrupted the meeting. "I've found it!" he exclaimed, causing the Elders to be taken aback. "I have found the solution to the issue of infertility!"

The Elders looked amongst each other in confusion and shock. The Chief Elder stands from his chair and begins to walk towards Elohim. Once there, he places his hand on Elohim's shoulder and glances down at Elohim's stack of notes, "Show us." He says warmly.

Elohim walks over to a table, and the others follow. He scatters his notes across the table and begins explaining his findings as the Elders listen and read what is before them. Questions are asked, answers are given, and by the end of the meeting, the entire council agrees that they must see if these new findings are truly the answer to their long-established problem.

A research team is formed within a day with Elohim as its leader. The team sets out for the newly found planet and arrives a couple of days later. Their plan was to set up a camp far away from the site of the fires and slowly make their presence known to the planet's natural inhabitants. Their hope is to gain the trust of these humans and learn their ways. All while trying to figure out how they procreate.

This process takes months, but it does happen just as the angels have planned it. The humans were scared and skeptical at first. It was quite shocking for them to see these advanced beings that looked similar as they did yet were so much more advanced than they were. But over time, they became trusting in the angels and showed them their way of life. The angels taught them their knowledge in medicine and construction, while the humans taught the angels how to survive in their lands.

Eventually, Elohim felt confident that the humans could be trusted and decided to tell them of the angel's strife. He met with their leaders and convinced them to allow some of their people to travel back to Eden to see if the two races could indeed procreate. A small group of humans volunteered to go, consisting of ten women and ten men. In exchange, Elohim agreed to permanently leave all the equipment the angels had brought, as well as leave a few angels behind for a short period of time to teach the humans how to use everything. Then those angels would return to Eden after.

Once the peaceful agreement was reached, Elohim, the returning angels, and the volunteers gathered up their things and began the trip back to Eden. Upon their arrival, the humans were warmly welcomed and provided sanctuary in the Temple of the Weavers. Over the next few days, samples were obtained from the humans and tests began running. Elohim, along with the other Elders, worked tirelessly comparing the humans' DNA to their own.

The DNA was strikingly similar but leagues apart as far as evolution was concerned. The other Elders were pleased by the similarities and wanted to move forward with live testing, but Elohim had his reservations. He got into several disagreements with the others, begging them to reconsider live trials. He asked for them to wait until the humans evolved for a closer match to be made. He was worried that if they attempted to procreate with the humans, the gap in their genetics would not be stable and that whatever was born from these trials would not be what they hoped for them to be.

But the Elders were impatient. They claimed that by waiting for the next step in human evolution, it would jeopardize the angel's future. Too much time would need to pass, and, in that time, the angels would diminish down to almost extinction. They declared, against all of Elohim's pleading, that live trials were to take place immediately.

Elohim felt defeated and betrayed. The Elders had trusted him enough to find a solution, but would not heed his warnings. He knew that eventually the humans would evolve into a more suitable match, but time was not on his side. He did not know exactly what would happen, but he did know that Eden was not prepared for it. He no longer felt as though he was suited to be part of the Council and removed himself from it. He set up a research lab in his own private dwelling and conducted algorithms to see what possible outcomes may take place.

To his dismay, all outcomes showed an unstable pairing. Just as he had feared, the instantaneous jump in evolution would genetically corrupt the host in many different ways. Even though he could not pinpoint what exactly the modification would do, he knew that he had to convince the Elders to not go through with the testing. He went to the temple and requested an audience with the Elders, but they refused him.

So, Elohim redirected his studies and began researching ways that could stop this impending doom. However, there were far too many variables to consider and not enough time to conduct tests on each. He knew that he was limited to a time period of eight to eleven months, which is nowhere near the time he needed to test his research. He knew what he needed to do, but struggled to bring himself to do it. He needed to create something so powerful that nothing in current existence would be able to stand against it.

For days, he struggled with an internal battle in his head and feeling crazy for thinking of such a harsh solution to a problem that had yet to exist. But the science was there, and so were all the results from his algorithms. He knew that he was correct, but still could not fathom the thought of wiping out all life from existence. He sat on the floor in the dark with the only light coming from his screens, staring at the results for hours. Finally, he took a deep breath and ran his fingers through his hair. "It must be done," he said to himself as he got up and began his work.

In the following days, Elohim made great progress on his secret plan. However, his sudden disappearance and lack of bothering the Elders was noticed. The Council had known Elohim for quite some time and knew he was not one to give up so easily. Concern was felt throughout the Council as fear of sabotage hung in the air. They held a special meeting and agreed to find Elohim.

Unfortunately, their fears were correct.

The day after their meeting, the Council burst into Elohim's hidden chamber. Before him lay the blueprints of a weapon vast enough to unmake Eden itself, its designs glowing on every wall. Their worst fears were confirmed. Elohim was labeled a traitor and was thrown into a secret, secluded prison far from the city's limits. He was the first angel to ever be imprisoned, and there he was held without access to anything other than bare necessities. Aside from food deliveries, Elohim was all but forgotten about. That is, until he was needed.

In the Beginning:
Part iii

onths went by, and the first generation of angel-human hybrids were born. These hybrids were given the name of Nephilim, and they all shared the same characteristics. They all grew jet black hair and had the same amber eyes as the humans. Their skin was fair enough to see their veins, and within those veins pumped sapphire blue blood.

At first, all seemed well. The Nephilim were born strong, their laughter filling Eden's halls. The Elders mocked Elohim's concerns, raising goblets in celebration, convinced the age of infertility had ended.

But these celebrations were short-lived.

The Nephilim grew faster than expected. They required more nourishment than what was originally thought, and became aggressive as they got older. When they became angry, their eyes turned bright white, and their blood turned black, which caused their skin to do the same. They would conjure up a tremendous energy that would allow them to move and manipulate things with their minds. They became highly intelligent, able to outsmart even the most advanced minds of the angels.

The angels were powerless against them and soon lost their position as the elite lifeform as the Nephilim overtook Eden. They began making it their own, using angels as slaves to do their work. A few militias were gathered, and attacks were launched in hopes of restoring the angel's power, but they all failed. These events caused the Elders to form a secret plan.

They had to free Elohim and help him finish his work.

They turned to a fellow Weaver named Sapien. He had been the one tasked with Elohim's care while he was imprisoned. The Weavers were aware that the two of them had been in communication throughout the years and felt that he would be best suited to convince Elohim to help.

Elohim was reluctant at first. He didn't feel as though the angels deserved to be saved, especially after the way they had treated him. He told them that they should have heeded his warnings, but instead they threw him in a cage and forgot about him. He was bitter to the Elders, but he eventually agreed to help because not all who were suffering were at fault.

With Elohim at the lead, they conducted missions to gather all that was needed to build their weapon. Sapien became Elohim's right hand and headed the secret operations while Elohim concentrated on his work. They moved not only under the cover of the shadows but also under the cover of the Nephilim's own inadvertence. They had to be cautious of those loyal to the Nephilim as well. One careless mistake would mean certain death.

Once everything was obtained, the work to eliminate the Nephilim began. Before his arrest, Elohim was already close to a final construct of the weapon. However, he and the Elders agreed that there must be a failsafe. There must be a way to not only undo what had been done but also a way to restore it to the time before the Nephilim were created. The question was, how?

So, a plan was set forth. They would simultaneously work on the weapon, which they had dubbed The Darkness and a way to counteract it, while also creating a way to bring it all back after the weapon was released. Through their testing, they found out that the darkness resisted the Pure Light that came from the energy of a nearby star. However, in concentrated doses, the light could burn away the Darkness, and in turn, a method of infusion was created.

To do this, Elohim and the others decided to take splices from their DNA, along with energy obtained from the brightest star, and infuse them into a vessel. Once the sustainability of the vessel was confirmed, they would shoot it into the farthest reaches of space. As it traveled, it would grow to perfection and then awaken. This vessel would have all the knowledge of the time before the Darkness and would seek to re-establish the universe as it once was. The vessel was named Lux-Signifer, meaning "Light Bearer."

The launch of this vessel would, without doubt, alert the Nephilim and their followers, causing them to seek out the secret order. During that time, all members of the order would fight off the Nephilim for as long as they could while Elohim readied the Dark Matter to be released.

The secret plan would eventually be discovered, and the order would fall. But they would die knowing that their lives had to be given in order to give the vessel enough time to get as far ahead of the weapon as possible. Elohim would be the last of his species alive in Eden. He would release The Darkness at the last possible moment, and once released, it would spread rapidly, and all life and light would cease to exist.

Elohim's last thought would be of the light bearer and the hope of its success.

Lux Signifer would later be who we now know as God, and he would awake in complete and total darkness. He would begin his life not only by having to fight but also having to create his own weapon against the Darkness.

We already know what the weapon and plan is. The question now is, will God succeed, or will he face the same outcome that his ancestors had?

Chapter
10

The Fall from Grace: Part I

We return now to our original story.

Michael stands across the pond from Lucifer as God makes his way over towards the mother and her children. He finds himself in a strange position where he is unable to foresee an outcome. To his right is his father, who, to his knowledge, has never led them astray. A father who has guided them and given them purpose, and never has given any reason for doubt in his efforts. Yes, he now knows that God has kept secrets, but that will need to be discussed later. For now, he must focus on the events before him.

Across from him, he sees Lucifer in a state of internal struggle. He knows his brother well, as Lucifer has been his mentor in times of God's absence. Lucifer was the one who taught him how to defend himself against the Darkness. In some ways, Lucifer had been more of a father to him than God. But Michael never held Lucifer as more respected than his father; that was just not his way. However, Lucifer had become different. He no longer seemed to be the fierce warrior that had once led them in battle. He appeared to have softened a little in his time away from the war.

Lucifer had always been the one to steady them. Michael remembered countless times when his brother had stood at the front of the charge, never demanding of them what he would not endure himself. He was always confident and never struggled to execute anything that needed to be done. So why was he struggling now? What had happened to Lucifer in this garden? And...

Something happens that breaks Michael's train of thought. For a moment, Michael sees Lucifer's body relax, almost like he paused. And then he immediately turned his head toward God. His eyes were all but aflame. Micheal instantly realizes what is about to happen, but he knows that he cannot act quickly enough.   His heart hammered as realization struck. He could not move fast enough, his limbs heavy as stone. All he could do was cry out..

"LUCIFER, NO!"

It makes no difference.

Lucifer lunged at God, closing the distance in a blink. The air cracked with force as his fist connected, sending God spiraling through the garden. He tumbles around trying to catch his footing, but before he is able to get back to his feet, Lucifer is on him once more, delivering a swift kick to his ribs. Again, God goes tumbling, letting out a groan of pain as he does so.

He lands on all fours this time as he hears Lucifer cry out, "You will not touch them!" His voice is different, lower, and deeper than normal. Lucifer again charges at him, but God has regained his composure and dodges the attack. As he rises to his feet, he turns around to face Lucifer and braces for battle.

Lucifer stands before him. He has unleashed his full fury as well as his light. It glows like yellow flames around him, and his eyes have turned golden. His wings are full spread and flowing with Pure Light. This is Lucifer's true form, the form that God created him to be as the perfect weapon against the Darkness. It is Lucifer's raw power infused with God's grace, but God never anticipated being on the opposite side of it.

But God does not back down.

By this time, the other four angels have flown over and created a barrier between God and Lucifer. They all face their brother and have braced for a fight.

Lucifer locks eyes with each of them before looking past them and into God's eyes. "I have no qualms with the four of you," he says, not breaking eye contact with his father. "But if you stand against me," he looks at Michael directly, "I will strike you down."

The four siblings look at each other, unsure of what their next move should be, for they are all in uncharted territory. But then God's voice comes from behind them.

"Stand aside children," he says calmly as he walks through them. "I will handle this."

The four do as they are told and encircle God and Lucifer. "No," God says to them. "Go secure the children."

Again, the siblings look at each other for guidance; however, Raphael does not hesitate. He starts walking toward Lilith, but in a flash of light, he is grabbed by the neck and hurled back as though he was weightless.

Lucifer moved so quickly that even God was unprepared for it. Lucifer then turns back to the group and states, "Anyone who attempts to harm the children will be destroyed. This is your only warning." He looks to his father, "Leave now. Forget about us and move on. There is no need for this."

God released a sharp, derisive hmph, his fury barely contained. "You disobey me. Break the trust of your siblings and strike me, and then expect me to walk away??! And what? Leave you here with your new little family?" He begins to pace back and forth. "Do you not yet realize what you have done? Why would I, a creator, want to destroy something?" He stops pacing and steps closer to Lucifer. "Think, Lucifer, throughout your entire existence, all I have done is create things to do what? Defeat the Darkness. And you have created the very thing that started ALL of this!"

God's face is flush with anger. "The Nephilim are the reason the Darkness is here! If left to live, they will bring forth a destruction far greater than even I could foresee! And you expect me to just walk away and sacrifice everything that we have worked so hard to accomplish? If this is what your thoughts truly are, then you have already been corrupted by them, and I will wipe you from memory." He snarls as he takes another step closer to Lucifer. "You, your children, and your whore."

Rage erupted from Lucifer, his aura flaring as flames of light roared around him. With a guttural cry, he hurled himself at God. He moves so fast that none of the archangels can react fast enough. Lucifer curls his fist and attempts a right hook to God's jaw. Even God is caught off guard, but is able to avoid the hit. He grabs Lucifer by the back of his head and slams him face-first into the ground.

The ground trembles as all the air from Lucifer's lungs is expelled, causing him to lie there in a daze. A crimson trail of blood starts to pool around his head. His ears are ringing, but he can hear Lilith's muffled voice crying out to him. How was he able to attack God before without God being able to deflect him?

Lucifer reaches back, grabs God's wrist, then tucks and rolls, pulling God down. He mounts God and delivers heavy hits before God kicks up and flips them both. God grabs Lucifer by the ankles and spins him around before launching him into the air. Lucifer spreads his wings, halting himself, before diving down to strike God again.

God anticipated the strike. His fist met Lucifer's face with such force that the sky cracked in thunder. The shockwave flattened trees and shook the garden to its roots.

Lucifer falls to the ground hard. He attempts to stand but cannot get his body to cooperate and falls back down. Slowly, the light begins to fade as he closes his eyes and passes out.

God stands over him contemplating whether he should end it here and now. Lucifer may have caught him off guard before, but that was only due to him being distracted. Memories of the two of them pass through his thoughts. He thinks about when he first created Lucifer. About when he first breathed life into him, and how, when Lucifer's eyes opened to meet his. He had been alone for so long that having someone else there gave him new strength.

Lucifer didn't ask even a single question. Like he already knew what he needed to do. He just stood next to God and joined the battle. The two never spoke a word to each other until after a victory was achieved, which was several years later. God thinks about their first conversation in their new light barrier and how Lucifer was only interested in coming up with ways to defeat the Darkness instead of asking why he was created. He never seemed to care about that aspect. He just served God and did as he asked.

God lets out a deep sigh as he looks around at the garden and sees how everything has begun to die. He is the only one who knows what death is at this point in time. No other being alive has ever seen death besides him. He hangs his head, questioning his decisions up until now. But he has no time to dwell on these thoughts. He must put things back in order as quickly as it can be done. The Darkness may have already found the garden, but it has not come in full force yet. There is still time, and he must act now.

He looks over to his other four children. Raphael has rejoined the group. The strongest angel is both visibly angry and physically hurt. It was no minor blow that he received; he had been thrown by Lucifer with nothing held back. It pains God, but he knows what he must do. He reaches down, grabs Lucifer by the back of the neck and lifts him up to look him in his closed eyes.

"I see now that I was wrong in choosing you." He says, disappointedly, as he throws Lucifer over to his siblings. "Bind him." He commands.

Without hesitation, Raphael walks over and picks Lucifer off the ground and carries him to an open and flat spot in the garden. Gabriel and Uriel begin to pull elements from the earth and garden and form them into chains.

Gabriel and Uriel are quick at their craft. Forging the chains as though their hands were knitting needles, and once completed, they drive the chains deep into the earth and seal the voids around them. The chain links are thick, heavy, and they are as black as obsidian. Raphael then sets Lucifer up onto his knees and binds him by wrapping the chains around Lucifer's wrists and waist, giving him little to no room to move.

Michael is off to the side and has not moved from where he was standing. The eldest of the four stands with his head hung low. "How has it come to this?" he asks himself. He can feel God's eye peering at him, but he does not care.

As his sister and brothers rejoin him, Uriel places a hand on his shoulder. He doesn't move his head, but he looks over at her. Even though she says nothing, her soft eyes tell him that she too, is in pain. Michael is about to say something, but Uriel averts her glance quickly and lets him go.

Michael senses God coming over. The other three angels take a step back and kneel, yet still Michael stands. God acknowledges the three with a nod, and they rise back to their feet. He then turns and stands beside Michael. There is a brief pause before God begins to speak calmly and fatherly.

"I know that I ask a task of you that is hard. It is hard for me to even ask it. But if we do not restore the order of things, it will be far harder to deal with what comes next than what lies before us now." He turns to Michael and lifts his head so that they are looking at each other. "Please do as I ask."

Michael searched his father's gaze and, beneath the fire and command, saw sorrow. It broke him to know that the same man who demanded such cruelty also bore the weight of regret. He then looks over to Lucifer, who is still unresponsive. Off to Lucifer's left is the woman. She is now holding both children in a protective grasp, her eyes widened by fear. Then he looks back at his siblings, who are all staring at him. He lets out a frustrated sigh before kneeling to God and asks,

"What do we do now, Father?"

"We must start again," God says somberly. "This garden and everything in it must be destroyed. The corruption has grown far too deep-rooted for it to be salvaged."

Michael's head snaps up to look at God. "Destroyed?!" he asks in shocked confusion.

"We do not have the time for me to explain." God snaps.

Michael's eyes widen. "Father, you can't mean..." God stops him mid-sentence as he turns to glare at him.

"It must be done," he says in a growling whisper.

God walks away from the four and over to where Lucifer is knelt. He kneels beside him and whispers in Lucifer's ear so that only he can hear what is said. "For reasons you will learn later, I cannot kill you. But I can make you suffer, the same as I am, for what you have done."

He then stands up and stretches his hands out in front of him, directing them towards the ground behind Lucifer. He closes his eyes and begins to focus, channeling all his energy. The earth starts to tremble, getting more ferocious with each passing second. Lilith quickly clammers over to the base of the tree and huddles down to protect herself and her children. The man throws himself over them, using his body as a shield. The four siblings kneel and brace themselves as hurricane-like winds begin to blow.

Dust and debris fly all around, smashing into the flower bushes, ripping them out of the ground. Michael shields his face as he peers through the storm. He can barely make it out, but he sees Lucifer still bound by his restraints, and God's hands are glowing bright white. God opens his eyes, now glowing the same as his hands, and lets out a powerful yell as he telepathically rips open the earth.

"EEEERRRAAAAGGGGHHHHHHHHHHHHHH!!!!"

And then.... stillness.

All those who were bracing for the storm look up and are in shock to find that a vast, seemingly bottomless pit has been formed behind

Lucifer. It stretches beyond what the eye can see, becoming wider the farther it goes. God, out of frustration, has fallen to his knees beside Lucifer but is facing the pit, and he is crying.

"Why, my son? Why have you put us into this position?" he asks an unconscious Lucifer, tears streaming down his face. "You are my firstborn. My right hand. Your light and strength are second only to mine. You were my first creation. We fought side by side and had the same goal. Never would I have thought that we would be here." He pauses to wipe his tears.

"I spent millennia working on and creating this plan. You and your siblings spent just as long trying to create these safe havens, and I chose yours because it was perfect for what was needed. A perfect energy source. A perfect vessel. A perfect garden."

Again, God pauses to collect himself. He looks into the pit that he had just created, then to the destruction that lies around. His heart is heavy as he again questions if he is doing the right thing.

A tense stillness hangs in the air as God stares into the void.

"It wasn't perfect," comes Lucifer's soft and faint voice, catching God off guard. He turns to look at Lucifer. "What did you say?" Lucifer lifts his head and looks at his father. "It was never perfect." Lucifer's lips twisted, not in joy, but in bitter defiance.

God rises to his feet, "What do you mean?" he asks, an angry tone filling his voice once more.

A smirk forms on Lucifer's face. "The man was infertile, unable to bear any children of his own."

God looks over at the man for a moment, then back to Lucifer. Even though anger sits on God's face, Lucifer can see in God's eyes that he did not know. "So instead of calling upon me so that I may have fixed this issue, you chose to impregnate the woman yourself?!" he snarls.

Infuriated, God looks over to Lilith, then to Raphael and Gabriel. "Bring them to me now," he demands in a deep growl.

The smirk quickly fades from Lucifer's face. Fear courses through his veins, hitting him in the gut as he realizes what is about to happen. He begins tugging and struggling in his restraints, screaming for his brothers to stop.

"NO! NO DON'T! DON'T TOUCH THEM!" Lucifer thrashed against the chains, the metal grinding as his voice tore through the air in desperation.

But Raphael and Gabriel continue despite Lucifer's pleas. Lucifer looks over to Uriel and Michael.

"PLEASE!" he begs, "DON'T LET THEM DO THIS!"

But the two remain stoic.

Gabriel arrives at God first, cradling both children. The living one is wailing while the other lies limp in his arms. Lilith is screaming and fighting with all she has as Raphael drags her over by her hair and the back of her head. He throws her down face-first in front of Lucifer and places his foot on her back, all while sneering at his bound brother.

The two lovers lock eyes, but each is filled with different emotions. She is full of anguish and fear. He is full of sorrow and remorse. For the first time in his life, he is powerless.

God has now taken the living child from Gabriel. "Michael," he calls, "come."

Michael is hesitant, but he does as he is told. When he arrives, God places the child into his arms. The infant immediately calms down and looks Michael in the eyes. It's eyes glowing like two ambers against a flame.

Behind him, God has picked up a flat rock. He hits it a few times, making pieces fall as he walks back over to Michael. He extends his hand and stares Michael in the eyes.

"Kill it."

Michael looks down and sees that God has crafted a blade out of the stone. His eyes widen as he hears Lilith start screaming. He looks at God in fear. "Father," he stammers, "It is but a child."

God stares at him coldly. "Do it," he demands as he pushes the blade toward Michael. "Or you will both die."

Michael's head is spinning. He turns and looks at Lucifer, who is looking back at him with pleading eyes. Lilith's screams turn into begging, causing Michael to make direct eye contact with her for the first time.

"Please, Michael," she says in a crackled voice. "Don't kill my baby."

Michael lowers his head and turns back to God. "Father, I have done many things for you, but this I cannot do."

"I understand," God says as he takes the child away from Michael.

"I am sorry, Father."

Michael barely has a chance to get those words out before God's blade carved from cheek to brow, searing across Michael's eye. A blaze of white pain exploded in his skull, and the world rang with the roar of his scream.

Michael drops to his knees, screaming in pain as he clutches his face. Uriel starts to rush over, but God screams at her, "LEAVE HIM BE!" causing her to stop in her tracks. God reaches down and lifts Michael to his feet. He pulls Michael's hand from his face and forcibly puts the child back in it. He shoves the blade into Michael's other hand and forces it closed. "This is your last chance."

Blood is streaming down Michael's face; his pain is unbearable. God has completely blinded his left eye. He looks at Lucifer through a cloud of blood in his good eye. It is at this point that Lucifer realizes the true gravity of their situation. He now can see that God has made up his mind and that nothing will stop him from destroying his family.

He stares back at his brother, who is bleeding heavily. Drops of blood fall onto the child, into its eyes and mouth, causing it to squirm and cry. The brothers have no need for words; they both are saying the same thing with their eyes.

I'm sorry.

God sees this interaction and grows tired of waiting. He grabs Michael's hand and thrusts the blade into the child's sternum. The child stops crying and lets out a tiny, surprised gasp. It then looks at Michael in pain and confusion. The two share a moment just staring at each other before the child reaches its small hand up, almost touching Michael's face, before exhaling its final breath and falling limp.

Michael's ears begin to ring as he falls to his knees, the stone blade clanking as it bounces off the ground. The distorted cries of Lucifer and Lilith can be heard as God pulls the child out of Michael's arms. Michael has been drained of all his energy, both physically and mentally, causing him to collapse into exhaustion. The last thing he sees before passing out is God tossing the lifeless child into the pit.

The Fall from Grace:
Part ii

Lilith's wails fill the airwaves of the Garden. The pain in her cries resonate through all in her presence. Lucifer stares at the pit over his shoulder in a paralyzed shock. An anger begins to rise within him, unlike anything he has felt before.

"RELEASE ME YOU FUCKING COWARD!!!" Lucifer screams, engulfed in his true form as he pulls against his chains, trying to break free.

Lilith is lying motionless on the ground now in a silent cry. Her tears have turned the dirt to mud, and it is now caked on her face. God walks over to Lucifer and slaps him across the face before grabbing him by the chin and saying, "I told you that I would make you suffer as I am."

He steps back and kneels beside Lilith, maintaining eye contact with Lucifer. "Tell me Lucifer, was she worth all of this?" he asks as he lifts Lilith under her arm and to her feet. "Was she worth the undoing of everything?"

Lucifer continues trying to free himself, but it's to no avail. God has begun walking Lilith around what is left of the garden. Uriel and Gabriel are tending to Michael as Raphael stares at Lucifer struggling. Almost as though he is getting enjoyment out of this.

God continues, "You should have just let me undo all of this. I would have done it quickly and without pain. I could have erased all of this from your memory so that you would not have to suffer as you are now." He pulls Lilith in closer. "She would not have had to have suffered the way in which she currently is."

Lilith has become numb. Her eyes are open, but her mind is not there. She has gone into full automation mode as God directs her around the garden. "I should let Raphael have his way with her before sending her into the void."

Raphael chuckles and turns to God. "Gladly," he grunts as he cracks his knuckles.

The sound of straining metal starts to fill the air, causing everyone except Lilith to look and see why.

Lucifer has once again ignited into his full power and has been able to plant one foot on the ground, giving it everything that he has in order to break free.

"YOU. WILL. NOT. TOUCH. HER!!!" He growls loudly as the sounds of the chains weakening grows louder.

Raphael quickly turns and punches Lucifer in the face as hard as he can, but Lucifer resists the blow. Hatred fills his eyes as he stares at his brother angrily, while Raphael's fist is still buried in his cheek. Though this temporarily stuns Raphael, he quickly brings his knee up and nails Lucifer in the jaw, snapping his head back.

In doing so, he breaks Lucifer's focus and causes him to fall back to both knees. Lucifer is breathing heavily as he spits out blood from his mouth. Again, he looks at Raphael.

"You'd better hope that I don't get free from these chains brother," he says. "I am going to unleash a wrath upon you that even the Darkness cannot bear."

"Your wrath means little compared to mine," God says, causing Lucifer to look up.

He is holding Lilith by the top of her head, her feet dangling above the ground. The pain from God squeezing her skull has brought her back to reality as she is clawing at his hands, trying to free herself.

"Do you love her?" God asks. "Do you love her more than your own life? More than your siblings?" God's eyes begin to glow. "More than me?" he growls."

All Lucifer wants to do at this moment is speak truthfully, but he knows that in doing so, Lilith's fate would be sealed. So, in the hopes of saving her, he relaxes his body, allowing his aurora to fade.

"You win Father," he says defeatedly. "Do what you will to me, but please," He looks to God with tears in his eyes. "Please let her go."

God's eyes dull as he looks at his fallen son. His arm even begins to drop as he contemplates what Lucifer has said. But in the very next instant, his eyes set ablaze again, and he raises Lilith up once more. "I asked you if you love this woman more than you love us! Answer me!"

"Yes," Lucifer whispers, knowing that there is no avoiding what is to come.

God's eyes widen slightly in disbelief. "Say it louder."

"I SAID THAT I LOVE HER!" Lucifer shouts back.

God lets out a deep, disappointed sigh.

"Then you are truly lost." His hand starts to glow, burning Lilith.

Lilith cries out and looks at Lucifer. "HELP ME!" she screams with an outstretched arm, trying to reach him.

Lucifer begins to cry. He knows that he cannot save her. He looks her in the eyes one final time. "I'm sorry," he cries. "I love you."

And then, in a flash of light, God disintegrates Lilith into nothingness. Her ashes slowly fluttering in the breeze.

90

Lucifer lets out a gut-wrenching wail of pain and sadness as he falls to the ground defeated.

In the midst of everything, Uriel was able to wake Michael up, but now she wished that she hadn't. All four of Lucifer's siblings sit in silence as they watch their brother writhing in agony. Even Raphael has become somber. He starts to feel remorseful as the reality of what just took place sets in.

God walks over to Lucifer and kneels while placing a hand on Lucifer's head. "Will you repent, my child?"

Lucifer's head hangs, his cheeks soaked in tears, allowing Lilith's ashes to stick to his face. The Earth trembles terribly, and rocks begin to lift off the ground and hover in the air. An ice-cold chill blows in as he begins to laugh a manic laugh. The sky begins to form black clouds, and red lightning pierces through the air.

God can feel a dark energy radiating from Lucifer. He quickly gets to his feet and scampers back as he takes in everything that is happening around him.

Lucifer's laughter continues as the storm rages, with each laugh becoming deeper and hollower. He has taken his true form once more, and the yellow fire around him starts to grow.

Suddenly, the yellow fire turns black with red embers, and Lucifer stops laughing. He slowly raises his head and unveils that his eyes are now crimson red as he locks eyes with God. "Repent?" he asks in a new raspy voice, chuckling while doing so. "Ha ha ha haaaa. No Father, it is you who shall repent."

God feels something that he has not felt since creating Lucifer.

Fear.

He quickly looks at the other angels. "We must leave now!" he shouts at them. "The Darkness has found us!"

The five of them gather close, getting ready to flee, but the storm has them surrounded. The Darkness rips and tears as it tries to consume them. The four angels unleash their inner light in an effort to fend off the Darkness, and God becomes his most pure form of light, glowing from head to toe.

"I'll hold it off!" he yells to his children over the rushing winds of the storm. "You need to escape!"

"FATHER!" Raphael yells as he points to Lucifer, "LOOK!"

God looks at Lucifer and sees the darkness spiraling into him at various points in his body.

"You asked me if it was worth it," he shouts over the storm. Lucifer spreads his wings and starts to rise, breaking the chains with ease. His skin has turned black, and two large horns are now curling upwards from his forehead. The black fire rages around his body. "It most definitely was," he says as he raises his arms, causing the storm to grow even stronger.

The group of five is forced to form an even tighter circle now.

"What do we do, Father?" Uriel screams.

God scans everything that he can, trying to find a solution. He sees that the pit is still open behind Lucifer and decides that there is only one option.

"No matter what, when I tell you to close the void, you close it," he says as he looks over his shoulder at his children. "Do you understand me?" The four siblings look at each other, then nod in agreement.

God shifts his focus back to Lucifer, who is now looking up and embracing his newfound power.

"LUCIFER!!!" he shouts.

Lucifer slowly tilts his head back down and looks at God, then begins speaking with evil on his tongue.

"I am no longer Lucifer," he thundered, his voice a chorus of many. "I am the Fallen One, Satan shall be my name, and Hell will follow with me." The sky blackened, the earth quaked, and even the angels felt fear pierce their hearts.

"Then fall," God says.

He leaps at Lucifer with such speed, it could not even be measured. He drives his knee deep into Lucifer's sternum while simultaneously grabbing Lucifer by the base of his wings and, with all his strength, pulls Lucifer's wings off. Crimson blood sprays out of Lucifer's wounds, soaking into the pure white feathers of his broken wings. The blow was so hard that the Darkness exited its host and burned away within the light of God and the angels.

Lucifer stares defeatedly at God before his eyes roll to the back of his skull, and his body plummets into the void below.

God hovers there holding the blood-soaked wings of his son as Lucifer disappears from sight. The farther he falls, the more the storm fades. Allowing the other angels to begin sealing the gap.

As God watches the void get smaller and smaller, he takes one last look at Lucifer's wings. "Goodbye, my son," he says before letting them slide from his grasp and into the pit, a lone tear dripping from his eye.

Chapter
11

Starting Again

Nearly a thousand years have passed since Lucifer's fall. God and the angels left the Forsaken Garden that day without saying a word to each other, for they were all lost in their own thoughts. Thoughts that were of no use trying to speak into words.

For the first time since Elohim released the Darkness, Death had shown its merciless face. God, having never witnessed death firsthand, was tormented by the fact that it was not the Darkness that took the first life in their war, but it was he who had. It affected him deeply, opening his eyes anew as to what now needed to be done.

His plan remained the same, but more safety measures needed to be taken. Through the consequences of what had transpired, God learned that the task of reproduction of souls was far too great for a single angel to take on alone. He would now charge two angels with the task of watching over the growth of mankind. However, in doing this, there was now a need for far more angels than the four he currently had. So, a plan of retreat and strengthening was launched.

God decided to pull the angels and himself back to the safety of their home. Their home that dwelled within the biggest and brightest star.

They had named this star Sanctuarium, and it was the first star ever created by God and the five archangels. Within it, they were able to create Hard Light. This type of light was created by condensing and pressurizing energy, giving it the ability to hold tremendous amounts of weight. This new technique allowed them to create floors, walls, and structures. They constructed a small manor. Each of them made their own quarters, connected to a main hall. They used materials harvested from the remaining gardens to furnish it, giving them a place to rest comfortably.

The angels' rooms consisted of beds, chairs, and dressers similar to those that you would find in an old cottage in the woods. It wasn't much, but it was better than nothing at all.

God had no use for a room to rest in, his energy recovered quickly when not in use. He did, however, have use for a workstation. Within the workstation, he crafted workbenches, tables, and tools. The very ones that he used to create the man, woman, and, of course, the souls.

In the center of the main hall stood a large table made from a plank of wood that came from a tree that no longer exists. The sides of it were live edged with veins of emerald running like a river through the cracks in the bark. The cambium layer was pale green in color, the sapwood was copper-toned, but the heartwood was the jewel of the piece. A thick strand of pure gold ran the length of the table straight down the middle and branched out into the sapwood.

This was their home, Sanctuarium, the first star. God knew that by retreating, the Darkness would claim more ground, yet the choice was forced upon Him. The decision weighed heavy, like surrender whispered against His will. The events that occurred in Lucifer's Garden showed him that there was a new threat aside from The Darkness.

Corruption.

If Lucifer could fall into corruption, then the others could fall even easier.

However, God would not let all their hard work go to waste. Within the safety of their star, the four angels would begin pulling from their inner light, and then God would weave their light in diverse ways in order to create an army of new, lesser angels.

They were formed of pure light, bodies that gleamed with radiance, minds alive with thought. Yet each was bound to God's own life force, tethered forever to His will and cause. This new army could be deployed in large factions capable of unleashing waves of light that would create an impenetrable barrier to the Darkness. This tactic could be repeated over and over until an equilibrium of light and dark was reached. Then a fully matured soul could be placed, eradicating the Darkness within the barrier. This tactic would be called, Dispelling.

However, this would require use of God's most limited resource, time.

After taking the necessary time for God to prepare and the angels to recharge, the plan was set into motion.

First, after the angels regained their strength, they sat in a circle around God, who was in his purest form. They then began pulling light threads from within themselves. These threads were like pieces of long, glowing golden hair that floated weightlessly through the air. God would then grab them and weave them into bodies. Once they were fully formed, these lesser angels would join the archangels and pull light from within them as well, adding to the pool of illuminated fibers. This went on for years until a large enough army was formed.

Secondly, God created two new souls and two new vessels. These vessels were thoroughly gone over and checked to ensure that they were indeed flawless. Once they were found to be perfect, they were placed into the garden that Gabriel had created and set on their path to procreate. Gabriel and Uriel were charged with watching over them.

This was due partly to it being Gabriel's Garden and him knowing it best, along with the needed care and compassion possessed by Uriel, and partly due to God needing his two strongest archangels, Michael and Raphael, to help train the lesser angels in dispelling tactics.

Once everything in Gabriel's Garden was set, the battle against the Darkness began to draw closer. In a few hundred years, enough souls will have been produced to wage a proper war, turning the tide, and completing God's task. All there was to do now was wait. But God knew that idleness breeds unrest. It would not be long before the ghosts of the past stirred once more in the present.

Chapter
12

A New Threat

In the years that it took God and the archangels to develop and begin their new strategy to defeat the Darkness, it had, in turn, spread farther and consumed much of what God had already secured. The Darkness had also evolved into an even more powerful form after Lucifer allowed it to use him as a vessel. It now had the ability to withstand pure light more than it was previously able to. Making it even more of a threat to God's crusade.

In the days after leaving the Forsaken Garden, and while the others rested, God and Michael met in private to discuss the events and decisions that were carried out.   God lowered his eyes and spoke softly, his hands clasped behind his back. He apologized to Michael for his harshness, yet his voice remained firm, refusing to yield on the reason why. He explained that during those events, he could not allow even the slightest of waivers from Michael or the others.

Even though he knew Lucifer was already lost, he'd much rather would have had Lucifer return to his grace, than what took place. He provided Michael with the insight of Elohim and the time before his creation and explained why he needed to use Michael as an example for what happens to those who disobey him. "They must fear me more than the Darkness," God said, his tone cold. Michael felt the words strike like ice, a truth that burned worse than the wound over his eye.

Though this was hard for Michael to hear, he eventually came to understand and forgave God for taking his eye. He requested that God tell him everything about Elohim, the first angels, and the Nephilim.

God was hesitant at first, but Michael convinced him by saying that the more knowledge he had, the better he could fight their enemy with. God swore Michael to secrecy and allowed Michael to transcribe it all.

Michael hesitated, then asked quietly, "How can you be sure these are memories, Father, and not visions?" God's gaze drifted to the void before he answered.

"This knowledge has come from somewhere beyond me, Michael. My own first memory was of waking up. When I did, I had no idea what was going on. I was just being attacked by the Darkness and had to fight." He looks off in thought. "These memories came to me over time."

"Are these memories Elohim's?"

"That, I am unsure of. But I know that somehow, he can be brought back, and this war will finally end."

Michael lays down his notes, stands up, and walks over to God. The two of them peer out into the void of space. Michael knows where his father's mind is at, and it isn't of the war.

"Lucifer is gone, Father. He will not return to us. But if you allow it, I will lead us to that victory."

God straightens his pose but does not look at Michael; he just speaks.

"You have my blessing. Go and tend to the matter of dispelling. I have something that I must do. When you are ready, call for me."

Michael bowed his head and walked away to begin his work.

Armed with new knowledge, Michael tempered himself like steel in fire. Years of discipline honed him into a warrior-scholar second only to God, a leader whose presence commanded reverence among angels.

He created a branch of the army which he named the Order of Michael. The Order consisted of the first and second generation of lesser angels. These angels proved to be stronger than the others, and Michael believed that was due to them being derived either directly from the archangels or a mix of the first generation with the archangels.

The Order contained two hundred and seventy-two highly trained lesser angels. Michael drilled them himself until they moved as extensions of his own will, a single tide of light flowing wherever his hands directed. Though their bodies were made of solid light, Michael had each of them wear the traditional white hooded robes. The Order was trained to move and act as one and only listened to Michael and God if necessary. This elite force acted as guardians of the souls and was only to be deployed during the final push before a soul was placed.

During the time of preparation, Michael had several meetings with Raphael and was able to guide him from being just a destructive force to becoming a level-headed war general who acted on proper judgment rather than solely on blinded aggression. Michael charged him with being the leader of the rest of the lesser angel army and gave him the task of leading the Dispelling. Once Raphael's forces pushed the Darkness back to a point of deadlock, Michael would lead The Order to achieve a final push back before God would place a star, securing that area and ridding it of the Darkness for good.

"At first, their campaign flourished. Under Michael's command, the angelic host carved corridors of light into the void, planting stars where only darkness had reigned for a millennium. Gabriel and Uriel were doing an excellent job of maintaining the garden and elevating the humans. Soon, hundreds of stars were scattered throughout the vastness of space.

With Michael and the others handling the proceedings against the Darkness, God was able to step away from the direct battle and shift his focus to coming up with a way to ensure that the light in the universe would never be snuffed out again.

But then one day, everything changed.

Michael was checking in on the latest star that had been placed, ensuring that it was stable, when Raphael called out to him telepathically.

"Michael!"

Realizing the concerned tone in Raphael's voice, Michael immediately stopped what he was doing. "What is it, Raphael?"

"Something is not right here," Raphael replied. "The Darkness is behaving differently than usual."

Michael turns his gaze in the direction of his brother's location, which was hundreds of thousands of miles away. "What do you mean behaving differently?" he asks. "It's not a living thing. It does not behave."

"Yeah, that's what I thought too," Raphael says. "You may want to come and take a look."

Knowing that his brother wouldn't toy with him on a matter such as this, Michael began heading Raphael's way.

It would take some time for him to arrive, but as he got closer, Michael started to notice that something was indeed off. When he reached the edge of the barrier, a terrible stillness awaited him. The air was cold, and the familiar hum of angelic light was gone, replaced by a silence that pressed against his chest. Raphael nor his angelic garrison were anywhere to be found.

Michael began to search within the perimeter for any signs of life. During his search, something off in the distance, past the light barrier, caught his eye. For a second, he swore that he saw a speck of light.

Michael stared intensely at that area, trying to see it again. "Has Raphael taken the army into the Darkness?" he thought to himself. No, he wouldn't do that. But where was everyone? He continued to stare at that spot, searching for something, anything to give him an answer. The more he stared, the more the Darkness seemed to ripple, shifting like a living tide instead of a void.

He leaned in closer to get a better look, but suddenly a hand came from behind him and cupped his mouth while pulling him back. The unknown assailant pulled them behind a nearby floating meteor before spinning Michael around, revealing that it was Raphael. While still cupping Michael's mouth, he held a single finger to his lips, motioning for Michael to stay quiet. Raphael crouched low, his armor streaked with deep scratches, his face pale and trembling. Blood shimmered faintly on his hands as he motioned for silence.

Speaking telepathically, Michael asks, "What happened?! Did the Darkness do this to you?"

Raphael doesn't answer right away. Trembling, he shakes his head as he peers around the meteor and into the abyss. "It wasn't the Darkness," Raphael whispered, his voice breaking. Michael followed his brother's stare into the abyss. "It was… it was…" The words died on his lips, swallowed by terror.

Chapter 13

Her

ichael could hardly believe what he was seeing. Off in the distance, where the Darkness thickened into a living wall, a figure hovered. Shadows coiled around her like a crown. Coal skin, amber eyes... She was nude and had dragon-like wings sprouting from her back, in between her shoulders. Her body was mostly covered in dark, iridescent scales except for her face and the front of her torso. Two large, twisted black horns rose from her temple area and stretched a foot above her head. They looked like the branches of a tree that had been burned. Her fingernails extended about an inch past the tips of her fingers, and she had a long, thick serpent's tail coming out just below her back that matched the color of her skin.

Though she looked entirely different from the last time that Michael saw her, there was no mistaking it. The woman in the dark was none other than Lilith.

She was holding her arms out and twisting her fingers, manipulating the Darkness around her. As the Darkness swirled, it unveiled a sight that shocked Michael and Raphael to their cores.

Dozens of members from Raphael's garrison were locked in twisted positions. Their limbs were in unnatural angles; their backs nearly spun the entire way around. Their jaws were unhinged and crooked, with their eyes rolled back in their heads. Darkness threaded through their bodies like worms in rotting earth, making their limbs twitch with unnatural jerks. The light within them flickered violently, pulsing once before dimming to black.

"What is she doing?" Raphael asks.

"She's turning them," Michael responds somberly.

The two brothers return to being fully behind the meteor. "What do we do?" Raphael asks.

"Tell me what happened," demands Michael.

Raphael looks at him in confusion. "There's no time for that; we must save them," he says as he starts to move.

"No," Michael says sternly, grabbing Raphael by the arm. "We saw what happened to Lucifer when the Darkness took root in him," Michael said, remembering his brother's blazing wings. "We are not ready for that fight."

Raphael relaxes, knowing that his brother is right. Michael looks him gently in the eyes and calmly says, "Tell me everything."

Raphael lets out a long sigh. "We were preparing to start another push into the Darkness. My angels were lining up to begin the dispelling process. However, this time the barrier wasn't as clean of a line as it normally is. It was like it was moving in and out, like it was pulsating." He looks at Michael. "That's when I called out to you."

Raphael continues. "I decided to have my men keep preparing while we awaited your arrival. They were almost set when these meteors began to cross the barrier," he pauses as he points to them. "We've seen these rocks floating around before, so we didn't think much of it at the time. But then we started hearing screams that were quickly muffled. I ordered the troops to hold and began searching to see what was happening. In the distance, I started to see some of the troops disappearing as the meteors were passing them."

He pauses a moment, recalling his memory. "That's when I first saw her. I didn't know that it was her at first. She clung to the shadowed faces of meteors, letting the Darkness cloak her as she stalked my men. As she passed one of my men, she made the Darkness reach out and grab them, sucking them beyond the barrier. Immediately, I called the troops to arms and led an attack on her. We fought hard, but she was too quick. It was like there were ten of her. She would be a hundred feet away, and then in an instant, she was right beside you. I soon figured out that she could teleport between the shadows."

He hangs his head. "But I figured it out too late, she had already taken a third of the men that I had brought. I called for us all to unleash our light in hopes of eliminating all the shadows within our barrier. Luckily, it worked. She fled to the equilibrium and began twisting the Darkness behind her, forming a storm much like Lucifer had. Then she released it in a devastating attack.... It was too powerful for the light of the lesser angels to withstand, and they were snuffed out instantly." Again, he turns to Michael. "The blast knocked me back, hiding me amongst the debris. Had I not been an archangel, I fear that I too would have been lost."

Michael places a hand on Raphael's shoulder. "I am glad that you were not, brother," he says with a smile. He turns and looks out at Lilith. "So now we know what her method of attack is. But what is her plan with the angels?"

"Soldiers?" Raphael suggests.

"Possibly, but for what?" Michael replies, looking at his brother before turning back to where Lilith was.

"I don't know, maybe to-"

Raphael suddenly stops talking, causing Michael to look at him again.

Raphael's eyes are wide, and he is struggling to breathe as he clutches at a thick black band that has appeared around his neck. Michael follows the trail of the band and realizes that it is a tail connected to a grinning Lilith who is hanging on to the top of the meteor. Her amber eyes locked onto Michael's as her tail coiled tighter. 'Hello, old friend,' she purred, lifting Raphael effortlessly.

Michael quickly distances himself and braces for a fight. "How are you still alive?!" he growls.

Lilith's laughter echoes around them, her grin changing into a smile. "We'll talk in a moment." She replies as she shifts her focus to Raphael. Her smile fades to a frown. "I have business with this one," she says as she tightens her grip and pulls him closer.

She attempts to fly back into the void, but Michael gets in front of her.

"Release him," he demands.

The two have a stare-down. It is obvious that neither of them are the same as they were when they first met. Lilith is sure that she could hold her own against him, but not while keeping Raphael in her grip. She realizes that this may not be a fight that she is ready for, so she slowly releases him, never breaking eye contact with Michael.

Raphael scampers back, holding his neck and gasping for air. Lilith then teleports back to the dark side of the barrier, where she and Michael continue their stare-down. She raised her arms slowly, and like puppets on strings, the twisted angels snapped upright, their movements jerky but obedient.

Michael takes a step back and helps righten Raphael. "Are you ok?" he asks.

"I will be," Raphael responds shakily.

"Good," Michael says as he scans the sight before him. "This is about to get tricky."

The corrupted lesser angels stand in a straight line in front of Lilith. A black goo sticks to them and flows around their bodies, allowing traces of light to shine through randomly, only to be covered back up again. They are slightly hunched over, twitching sporadically as though they are receiving an electric shock.

110

On the other side of the barrier, Michael and Raphael stand poised for battle. Both understand that this is an enemy with unknown abilities. And even worse, they do not know to what extent the hold is that Lilith has over them. Does she control only their minds, or their bodies completely? One thing is certain though; they must eliminate this new threat before it has a chance to grow.

As the standoff continues, Raphael starts speaking telepathically to Michael. "Do we call for reinforcements?"

"No. Not yet." Michael replies. "We may not know what they are capable of, but we do know that she can turn them. We need not risk adding to her numbers."

As if on cue, Lilith raises her right arm in front of her and flicks her wrist forward, pointing a sharp nail at the brothers. The moment that she does this, the Corrupted begin moving forward.

To Michael and Raphael's shock, the corrupted angels lurched into the light. Each step pulled shadow like tar behind them, their bodies trembling as if every inch forward was a battle against invisible chains. But they seem not to care and continue pressing on.

The brothers look at each other for a moment, realizing at the same time the danger this poses. Somehow, the Darkness has found the ability to fight within light. Knowing that they must act quickly, they charge the enemy. They attempt physical attacks but quickly find out that contact with the goo burns and eats away at them like acid. So, they switch to using their light to push them back. At first it has little affect, but as they make their light brighter, it forces the Corrupted to shield themselves and back away.

Michael yells over to Raphael, "Unleash your full light, Brother!" Together, the two become their pure forms. Golden flames engulf their bodies and their eyes glow with pure light. With wings outstretched, they extend their arms, causing orbs of light to grow around them. In doing so, the Corrupted start acting as if they are burning and quickly retreat into the safety of the Darkness.

Michael and Raphael allow the light to dull but remain in their pure forms. As soon as they do, the Corrupted begin crossing the barrier once again. It is apparent that they will not be stopped unless they are killed.

"We're going to need help," Raphael says to Michael.

"No." Michael refuses again.

"Michael, what are we to do? We will remain deadlocked if we don't have reinforcements." Raphael says, notably frustrated.

A wicked and cackled laugh breaks their concentration. It seems to be coming from all around them. They realize that Lilith is no longer on the other side of the barrier. Dark is cast over them from behind. They turn around to see that a large meteor has come between them and the star, creating a long shadow that extends into the Darkness. Lilith crawls out of the shadow, intimidatingly slow with an evil grin.

Feeling a chill at his back, Raphael turns back around to see that the Corrupted are charging through the shadow, directly at them.

"MICHAEL!!!" he screams, but it is too late.

Immediately, the two of them are surrounded by the enemy. The Corrupted rip and slash at them, burning their skin. Again, the brothers ignite their light, pushing their enemies back.

That's when Lilith makes her move. She lunges and Raphael, seemingly unbothered by the light, spins around rapidly and smacking him across his chest with her tail. This knocks Raphael back and causes him to let out a groan of pain.

Before he could recover, Lilith was upon him. She seized his head and drove her knee upward with a sickening crack, blood spraying into the void. She raises her hand about to claw away at him, but is suddenly yanked back and thrown. As she flies through the air, she looks back and sees Michael staring her down, fiercely.

Raphael screams, breaking the stare down, and causing Michael to look over and see him being attacked once more by the Corrupted. He pauses as he contemplates whether the decision that he is about to make is the correct one, but his brother's screams of pain make it for him. He looks off in the direction of Gabriel's Garden.

"Uriel. Gabriel. Come to me." Then he shifts his eye slightly to the left. "I call to The Order. Your leader needs you." He then turns, igniting himself again as he charges over to rescue his brother.

Michael erupted in blazing light, his wings slicing through shadow as he tore the Corrupted from Raphael like thorns from flesh. Raphael is covered in lacerations now and wincing in pain.

"That's some pretty wicked stuff they have on them," he tells Michael.

"We must stand back-to-back so that they cannot divide us," Michael commands. "Our siblings and The Order are on their way. We have to survive until they reach us.""Understood," Raphael says. "I just hope that they hurry."

"As do I," Michael says as he locks eyes with a grinning Lilith once more.

Chapter

14

A Lost Light

Panting. Heavy breathing. Growls and wails. Screams and laughter. The void vibrated with sound, each echo slamming against Michael's chest like a drumbeat of war.

These are the sounds that fill the battlegrounds as Michael and Raphael defend themselves against a seemingly never-ending onslaught. Every time they repel their enemy back, they immediately pursue again. All while Lilith lands sneaky blows, cackling in joy as she does so. Driven to desperation, the brothers darted between shadows, striking like lightning before retreating to narrow shafts of light, wings scraping against the jagged stones.

Throughout the fighting, Lilith has been able to entrap them inside a large circle made from asteroids and meteors. This caused most of the light to be blocked and only allowed a few slivers to pass through the gaps between the large rocks. The brothers were aware of her doings and had no option but to allow it due to the pursuit of the Corrupted. They were now primarily fighting within the shadow of their own star.

"Michael..." Raphael is speaking through labored breaths. "I don't know how much longer I can fight."

They are standing back-to-back within the safety of a light sliver, trying to catch their breath. Ralphael's robes hang in shreds, his golden light flickering. Each breath rattled as Michael shielded him, forced into defense instead of command. A smart move by Lilith. And though Michael has barely sustained any injuries aside from a few scratches and hits, he too, was becoming tired.

"Hold steady, brother. Reinforcements will be here soon." Michael assures him, hoping that he is right.

The Corrupted have found them again and are heading their way. Slowly, the light that provided them with sanctuary begins to fade as Lilith continues her entrapment plans.

Michael's eyes flicked between his faltering brother and the shadow where Lilith lurked. His fists clenched. Time was running out. Does he put himself between Raphael and the Corrupted? This would allow Michael to take on the many enemies, but pit his brother against Lilith, who would easily have the upper hand. Or does he take on Lilith and risk losing Raphael to the Corrupted? In Raphael's current state, it wouldn't take long for them to bring him down with their superior numbers.

Neither option favors them, causing anger to also blend with the other emotions that Michael is currently feeling. But sometimes anger is good to have in battle, and he uses it to fuel his drive. He starts to scan the battlefield and the asteroid circle, devising a plan. He then looks over his shoulder at his brother.

"Can you give me fifteen seconds?" he asks.

Raphael gave a cracked smile, a laugh escaping his bloodied lips. "Yeah, but it's not going to fare well for me, is it?" Michael's hand tightened on his shoulder, his first smile in hours. "I'm afraid not."

Again, Raphael laughs. "Alright then, what's the plan?"

Michael resumes scanning the asteroid circle. "On my go, you need to make yourself as bright as possible. You'll know what to do then."

"Understood," Raphael responds as his smile turns into a more serious expression.

Finally, Michael finds what he's been searching for. It is hard to make out, but he has undoubtedly found her. Lilith is clinging to an asteroid directly in front of the star, hiding within the darkness that's being eclipsed.

"Now!"

Michael planted a foot against Raphael's braced form and launched himself forward, hurling his brother toward the Corrupted as he rocketed at Lilith. The blinding light allows him to reach her before she even has a chance to realize it, seizing her by the throat. Lilith's eyes widen in shock as she clutches his wrists, trying to wrangle herself free. Michael tightens his grip and begins lifting Lilith from the rock, only to slam her back into it. Each slam cracked the asteroid like brittle glass. Shards floated into the void as ultraviolet light bled through the widening fractures.

"I've had enough of this!" he screams as he slams her the hardest yet. This causes the asteroid to explode into thousands of pieces and flood the shadow trap with ultraviolet light.

The Corrupted scream in pain as they quickly seek out darker areas, leaving Raphael alone and without a second to spare. The mighty Raphael falls unconscious, fully drained of all his energy.

Michael floats in front of the star, still clutching Lilith in his hand. He has never been angrier than he is now, and Lilith can surely see it as the panic in her eyes now turns to fear.

Michael's eyes blazed, his grip trembling with fury. "One way or another, you will tell me how you came back, how you did this, and how to undo it," he growled, dragging her toward the star's merciless heat.

Lilith may be able to withstand and fight in the light, but she is not capable of withstanding the pure energy of a star. Her back begins to burn hotter the closer they get. She tries to whip Michael with her tail, but he catches it with his free hand and continues moving them closer. Lilith begins screaming in agony as the skin on her wings starts to boil.

Michael is flooded with anger and has blocked everything out aside from extracting an answer. He cares for nothing else as his anger turns to rage and consumes him.

Behind him, wings of light tore through the darkness as Uriel, Gabriel, and The Order descended. But Michael's rage blinded him, their voices a distant murmur. Suddenly, he is snapped out of his trance by Gabriel grabbing him and pulling him away from the star.

"MICHAEL?!" Gabriel shouts. "What are you doing?"

Michael blinked, the haze of rage lifting. Only then did he see Lilith's scorched wings, the blisters rising on her skin, and felt a stab of shame. He gasps and lets her go as he looks around. Uriel is tending to Raphael, and The Order has formed a blockade around them all. Gabriel is now examining Lilith and looks to Michael for an explanation.

"Is this who I think it is?"

Michael is looking at his hands, which have also been singed. "It's the woman from Lucifer's Garden," he responds. Still in a bit of confusion himself. "I was trying to find out how she did all of this."

Gabriel looks around before replying. "Well, it's a good thing that we got here when we did. Otherwise, there wouldn't be anything left to give you an answer."

Uriel flies over with a now barely conscious Raphael draped over her shoulder. "What is going on here?" she asks.

"Raphael sent word to me stating that there was something strange happening in this sector. When I got here, there was no one to be found but I, too, sensed something was off. Raphael found me and showed me that what was left of his troops were beyond the light barrier and being corrupted by her," he says as he points to Lilith. "We were given little time to figure things out before she attacked us. It was then that we found out that the corrupted angels were under her control and that they were able to penetrate through the light barrier and fight in both light and darkness." He looks at Raphael. "Raphael was the primary target it seems, and he took the brunt through most of the battle."

Michael pauses as he looks out to the edge of the light where the Corrupted have gathered in wait. "They are capable of fighting in the light, but it is a strain to them. It's like the Darkness is pulling at them the entire time. Lilith moved these asteroids around while we were dealing with the Corrupted and trapped us in a shadow where the Corrupted could all but move freely."

He looks at the pieces of the shattered asteroid floating around. "I was able to get us free by breaking apart a section of the barrier and allowing pure light to enter." Looking at Gabriel, he continues, "You arrived while I was seeking an answer from her."

Michael, Gabriel, and Uriel all turn to look at Lilith, but are shocked to find that she is no longer there. A hard cough and sputtering are heard coming from Raphael.

Michael turns to see a smiling Lilith staring at him from over Raphael's shoulder, opposite of the one Uriel is holding him up by. Lilith quickly moves her eyes down and back up again, signaling Michael to look down.

As he looked down, time slowed. Lilith's blood-slicked hand protruded from Raphael's chest. Raphael gasped, eyes wide, blood flecking his lips. He looks back up at Lilith in utter shock as she winks at him and disappears.

"NNNNNNNOOOOOOOO!!!!" Michael screams as the others realize what has just happened.

Michael rushes over to Raphael as an epic battle ensues. One by one, Lilith begins picking off members of The Order, much like she had done with Raphael's lesser angels. Gabriel and Uriel join the fight but soon realize that it was just as Michael had told them and begin calling for a retreat.

All of that is background noise as Michael remains focused solely on his brother. Tears are falling from both of their eyes, and Raphael holds Michael's hand.

"I was better, right, Michael?" Raphael asks as he looks up at his older brother.

Michael pressed their foreheads together as Raphael's light dimmed like a dying star. "You were... You very well were."

Raphael smiles at him, "Finish this." He squeezes Michael's hand harder. "Finish this," he says again as the light fades from his eyes, and he falls lifeless.

With great remorse, Michael carries Raphael over to a nearby asteroid and lays him down softly. He closes Raphael's eyes and folds his arms across his chest to cover the hole that was made by Lilith, then stands up and looks over his now deceased brother. The battle rages behind him, but Michael remains in his own world. He is unfazed by what is going on and ignores the calls for help. He has only one thing in mind.

Finding Lilith.

He scans and searches, trying to locate her. He catches glimpses here and there, but she is moving quickly. She pauses only when she carries a body into the Darkness. Michael weighs his options. He isn't sure if his light can burn bright enough for him to withstand the Darkness, but he is sure that is the only place that he can get to her now. He looks back at Raphael.

"I will finish this, my brother."

Then he turns back and prepares himself to fight once more.

He is just about to fly off when suddenly, a shrill, piercing sound shoots through the battlefield, followed by a massive explosion of light, causing everyone to stop fighting. The Corrupted reel in pain and return to the safety of the Darkness. Lilith stops manipulating the Darkness through the newly gained angels and adverts her eyes away from the light.

Then the entire area falls silent.

Michael feels a familiar hand on his shoulder. He turns his head and sees God standing beside him. Together, they both look back at Raphael.

"Father, I..."

But God holds a finger to his lips, stopping Michael from completing his sentence.

"It is not your fault," God says as he continues to stare at Raphael's lifeless body. "Gather your brother's body along with your siblings and what is left of The Order and return home," he commands.

God turned to face Lilith. Maintaining eye contact as he hovered over to the edge of the Light. The angels froze, the Darkness itself shivering at his light. And then, to their disbelief, he crossed the barrier.

The Darkness immediately swirls around, trying to get to him, but God's light is too bright for it to penetrate. God walks right over to Lilith and gazes down on her.

Lilith, though caught off guard, stands her ground.

After a moment, God speaks. "Tell Lucifer that if he seeks revenge, not to send his puppet to do his bidding," he growls through clenched teeth.

Lilith glares coldly back at God. "I am not Lucifer's puppet. I act on my own accord." She replies boldly.

Unwavering, God leans down to meet her eye to eye, the Darkness still raging around him. "Do you?" he asks before straightening himself back up.

A slight smile forms on Lilith's face. "I do," she says as she raises her arms up, causing the Darkness to stop storming around God and fall in line behind her. In doing so, she unveils that not only does she now have a small army of corrupted lesser angels, but also an entire legion of shadow creatures that have been waiting under the cover of the Darkness.

These shadow creatures have dog-like legs and long, bony arms with twisted spikes sprouting from their elbows. These arms hang as low as their feet and have long fingers attached to their hands. Three-inch-long claws grow from each finger. Their skin, an ash grey color with a black smoke-like substance rising from their bodies. They have short snouts with razor sharp teeth, pointed ears, and black manes running from the top of their heads and down their backs. Bright red eyes glow within their sunken sockets. And there are thousands of them.

God looks around in horror at the sight of this all. Sensing the danger that was now before him, he quickly unleashes his inner light and retreats to the safety of the star's light. Lilith tilts her head back and begins laughing hysterically as the full force of her Dark Army charges the barrier.

He then looks to his children with fear in his eyes. "We need to go, NOW!"

He, Michael, Gabriel, Uriel, and a few members of the Order begin to fly away at the speed of light, with no choice but to leave the rest of The Order behind as they are consumed by the Darkness. The sound of Lilith's manic laughter trailed in the distance.

Chapter
15

An Unlikely Decision

They returned home in silence, wings heavy and eyes downcast. The air inside the hall trembled with the weight of loss; even the stars beyond the windows seemed dimmer.

God stands by himself, facing away from the angels. He chose to retreat after Lucifer, but this time, he was forced to. The Darkness has become tamed. How has she achieved this? He asks himself repeatedly.

Michael leaned over the table, his braids falling like a curtain to hide his face. His fingers trembled against the wood as he stared at Raphael's lifeless body, light flickering weakly from his palms. He is mournful over the loss of his brother, but he is also overcome with anger. Anger at the situation and at himself.

Gabriel sits with his back against a wall. His legs are bent with his feet planted on the floor, and his arms rest on top of his knees. His head is tilted back as he stares up at nothing while pondering if he could have done something more to save his brother.

Uriel is pacing back and forth rapidly. It is easy to tell that she is overwhelmed by scattered thoughts. She is the first to break the silence. "Can anyone explain what happened back there?" she asks as she takes turns looking at the others. "Anyone?" she asks again. This time, the frustration can be heard in her voice.

"She won," Gabriel says sorely. "She played us, and she won." He looks over at Michael, then to Raphael. "I should have just let you push her into that star."

A moment of silence passes before Uriel speaks again.

"But how is it her? We watched her dissipate into nothing. Now she's back and not only with an army, but also with the ability to control the Darkness? How?"

"I am unsure of the answer to your first question. However, the answer to your second question is a simple one," says God, now knowing the answer to his own question. "Just as I am a vessel for the Light, she has become the vessel of the Darkness. Where I contain my Pure Light and only unleash it, when necessary, she allows it to flow through her freely, manipulating it as she feels fit." His voice trails as he looks off in thought. "Until now, I believed that life could only be brought by the Light. However, we now know that it can come from within the Darkness as well."

"That which is born from the Darkness is not alive," Michael says loudly, his voice crackling a bit from being silent for so long.

The others turn and look at him out of confusion. "How can something born from death be alive?" He says as he struggles to stand up straight, still weakened from the fight. "We all saw it. We all saw our father turn her into something less than ash."

Michael staggered like a newborn fawn, his strength fraying with each step as he steadied himself against the wall. Clearly struggling from exhaustion, he uses any solid surface within reach to steady himself. "We were all there that day," he says as he looks at each of them individually. "You. You. And you. And... and..."

Michael looks at Raphael. "And you," he says as a tear rolls down from his eye. He takes a deep breath and collects himself. "Death brought her back for some reason. And death does not give life, it takes it." Michael looks at his father directly. "Something else is at work here. Something that we've been blind to thus far."

God fell silent, Michael's words echoing in his mind. Without a word, he crossed the hall to the soul-forging station, where countless orbs pulsed with quiet light. He picks one up and begins to roll it gently around in his hand before clenching it and delivering the same force that he had done to Lilith that caused her to disintegrate.

In a flash, the soul disappears into nothingness. Or so it seemed.

God peers closely at his hand. In it are billions of microscopic black particles, nearly unnoticeable unless searched for. He cups his hands together and delivers a flash of light within them, then opens his hands again to examine. To his surprise, the particles are now glowing with light and are moving. They speed up and get closer and closer together before creating a flash of their own, causing God to look away.

When God's eyes adjust, he is holding the very soul that he had destroyed minutes before.

"A soul cannot be destroyed," he whispered. Around him, the angels' wings rustled as if stirred by a sudden wind.

The angels have joined him now, in awe of what they have just seen.

"When the vessel dies, they go dormant." God rolls the orb around in his fingers." But when introduced to pure light, they wake up again."

"And what if they are introduced to the Darkness?" Gabriel asks.

God stares into the soul as he responds. "The orb we see before us is perfectly formed, a perfect sphere. If you were to draw a line through any point of this orb, it would be the perfect balance of Light contained within that line, no matter where you drew it."

He shifts his head in thought.

"But if the Darkness were to charge it, the particles would act individually and unformed. It would be unbalanced. It would be like containing a brewing storm into a tiny ball and chaos would ensue. It would corrupt whatever vessel the orb was inside. Allowing the Darkness to flow freely through it."

They all look at each other as each of them realizes what that means and says the same thing. "Lilith"

Gabriel sits back into a chair. "The darkness was all around us that day. Flowing right on through ol' Lucifer," he says as he cuts his hand through the air.

Uriel nods her head as she recalls that day as well. "She died while she was full of pain and agony. Her soul already would have been restless and easily corruptible."

God places the soul back down. "It matters little now. We know our threat and need to defeat it with haste. How many angels do we have here?"

"A few hundred? Maybe more." Gabriel responds.

"It will need to do," God says. "I want you and Uriel to take half of them and return to the garden to protect it. Michael, I want you to take the remaining and protect our home." God says as he appears to be prepping to leave.

"Where are you going?" Uriel asks.

God pauses. "To get the only thing that knows more about the darkness than we do." He turns and locks eyes with her. "Your fallen brother."

Gabriel and Uriel staggered back, jaws slack, their eyes darting between each other and their father as if words had abandoned them.

"Are you absolutely out of your mind?!" Michael exclaims. "Your answer to our problem is to bring here, the very being that started this all? The first one to allow the Darkness to consume him through his own free will?!"

"Exactly," God responds, slightly irritated. "He knows how to control the Darkness. It's just as you said, we were all there, we all saw it." God starts to walk towards Michael. "If I were to somehow convince him to help us, we can turn the tide back on our side."

Michael steps towards God and leans in. "Convince him how, Father?! What could we possibly have to offer him that would sway him to go against her?! To join the ones who murdered his family and turned their backs on him? Why would you even think that this is a possibility?"

He hesitates for a moment. "What if there was another way? Another way and you didn't have to make this journey? We just need time."

"Time is not something that we have, Michael," God replies.

"If we had another solution, would it not be worth taking the time?"

"No."

"Why? Why are you so set on releasing Lucifer?"

"BECAUSE IT IS THE ONLY WAY TO GET US OUT OF THIS HELL!!!" God thundered, his light flaring as he loomed over Michael. Michael flinched but held his father's gaze, jaw set. "Trust me, I am not sure of this option either, but we have no idea of how quickly Lilith may attack again or what the attack could even be, for that matter. This is our quickest option."

Michael steps back and begins rubbing his temples with his hand. "Then I'm coming with you. There's no telling what else lies out there or what Lucifer may have conjured up."

"No," God replies "You will not survive the journey. Especially as you are now."

"Then give me time to rest, and then we'll leave."

God places a hand on each of Michael's shoulders and smiles. "I appreciate your concern, my child, but even if we had the time to spare for you to rest, you still would not make it. I need you here, and I need to do this on my own."

Normally, Michael would have knelt. But sensing not a commander but a father before him, he reached out and placed his hands on God's shoulders, a gesture of both defiance and devotion.

"You better come back." He says as he fights back tears.

"I will," God promises as he pulls Michael in, hugging him tightly.

Gabriel and Uriel join them, and God kisses each of their heads. He then pulls away from them and begins walking to the exit.

"Take care of Raphael's body, then do as I have commanded you. I will return soon. Have faith, my children. I love you." His voice softened. Around him, the angels lowered their heads, their lights dimming in shared grief.

Then he turns and walks out of the room, leaving his children behind for the sake of all creation.

Chapter 16

The Descent

God crossed through empty worlds where stars flickered and died, the Dark Army's shadowy claws scratching at the edges of creation. He knew that it would be a hard trip, but even he was not fully prepared for the numbers that Lilith held.

He was not only spending his energy trying to keep the Darkness at bay, but also by fending off the shadow creatures. He could feel himself growing weak. The Darkness was already hard enough to deal with, but throwing in the constant berate of the Dark Army made it nearly impossible. However, God was glad that he had made Michael stay behind, for there was no way that he would have survived this.

His mind paused, heart racing. For the first time since the dawn of time, the question flickered through his mind: would he survive this?

God had begun to question himself. He had never driven himself into the Darkness. He had only ever pushed it back. To put it into a clearer perspective, it was like God was fighting inside of a powerful tornado at the bottom of the ocean while randomly being attacked by vicious sharks.

Still, he pushed on; failure could not be an option.

The trip that had once taken him mere minutes to make, was now taking days. God had started to think that he was lost. He knew that he was heading in the right direction when he left, but he feared that he may have been turned around by the storm and attacks.

He pressed on blindly, his inner light flickering, clutching at fading memories of the Garden to guide him.

And then, the storm subsided, and God found himself free of it.

To his front, was a vast, open realm. It was dark, but it was not the Darkness. More like a moonless night's dark. Behind him, the storm writhed, tendrils of shadow stretching like hands to drag him back, yet halting at an unseen boundary. Identical to the way it acted at the edge of the light barrier.

As his eyes adjust, God sees chunks of rock floating all around. He finds one suitable for him and lies down on it, finally able to rest. He looks up and is pleasantly shocked to see stars. They are lightyears away, but they are clearly visible.

This sight is a somewhat familiar one. He sits up and surveys the area around him.

The realm is a perfect sphere, twelve hundred miles in diameter. Small fragments of blackened rocks are scattered around the outer rim and gradually get larger the closer to the center that they are. Directly in the middle, is a large solid landform approximately two hundred miles long and sixty miles wide.

"Could it be?" God asks himself as he moves closer to the center. He gently weaves in and out of the floating rocks, doing his best not to disturb them but also examining them as he passes.

They are wrought with decay. Undoubtedly, The Darkness had passed through them.

As God continues his path, he notices something that is out of place. There, floating alone with no rocks around it, is a dead tree.

It is dried up and has turned black, and its branches are brittle with lifeless roots still clinging to it.

It is unmistakenly the apple tree from Lucifer's Garden.

God looks in the direction of home and locks eyes with the brightest star.

"Michael," God calls out telepathically, "I have found it."

"Father!" Michael happily exclaims. "Thank goodness, we thought that we had lost you."

"I am okay," God replies. "I'm almost to him."

There is a pause before Michael responds. "Be careful," he says deeply.

God landed on the edge of the landmass. Ash and decay stretched for miles, and the air smelled of a drowned campfire. In the silence, even his heartbeat seemed too loud.

Stillness. Total and complete, stillness.

Dried out remnants of the once lush plants are scattered about the garden. God walks over to the edge of a small crater and peers down into it as if he is expecting to see his reflection. It is all that is left of the pond.

Is this the same fate that was suffered by the people of the time before him?

Moments go by as God ponders that question before he snaps out of that thought and refocuses on finding Lucifer.

Using the pond as a marker, he begins to walk in the direction of where he had ripped the earth apart. He searched the dead garden for any shift in the terrain until he found a slight rise where the air felt heavier, humming faintly from below. God stands directly in front of it and looks around. To his right and left lie the half-buried remnants of the chains that once held Lucifer.

He stared at the ground, visions tumbling through his mind, Lucifer waiting, Lucifer gone, Darkness pouring out like a flood. Was he ready?

Is Lucifer still down there, and if he is, is he alive? Did he pull some of the Darkness in with him, and does it lie in wait? Has Lucifer remained as that which he had become before God condemned him? Is God prepared for these scenarios?

God has no choice but to put these fears behind him. He kneels down, grabs the ridgeline, and begins pulling it apart. This causes the earth to rumble and shake, leading to the falling of anything that remained upright on the surface. With a strained groan, he rips the earth open, then quickly braces himself for attack.

But as above, so below.

After the earth stops shaking, the complete stillness resumes, and the silence falls once more. God looks down into the abyss, waiting, watching, and listening. Minutes passed. The abyss yawned below, silent. God's light dimmed a fraction as dread settled over him. If Lucifer was gone, all was lost. "I need to be sure," he thinks to himself. He then levitates off the ground and slowly begins his descent down into the void. Unaware of what would be waiting for him at the bottom.

Chapter 17

Reunion

The faint light from above dwindled to nothing as God sank into the void. Shadows pressed close, muffling even his heartbeat. This was not the Darkness, but a place where light itself had fled. Even God's luster cannot overcome it. He is but a single candle in a long, dark hallway.

Eventually, he reaches the bottom. The void has narrowed to a point where God can extend his arms and touch the sides. The earth is cold against his palms and fingers as he runs them along. Feeling his way around all but blind, he starts walking. He remains on high alert, but the only thing he can hear are the sounds of his own footsteps.

He walks for hours like this, with the only difference being that the path has widened to a point that he can no longer feel the walls. Still, he continues wandering around in the barren desert that is devoid of sound and light.

Time lost all meaning as he walked. Only when his breath began to mist and ice glittered underfoot did he realize how long he'd been wandering. He walks further, cautiously excited by these changes. Then he hears something that makes him stop and lean in to make sure that he has indeed heard it. "Are those whispers?" he asks himself. Again, he presses on, and the whispers become clearer.

Whispers swirled around him like a storm: 'Why are you here… you are not welcome… no place for the light…'

"You should not be here."

The voices seem to be coming from nowhere and everywhere all at once, swirling around God.

Then he sees it.

A single thread of silver light rose from the abyss, as delicate as spun glass yet steady as a pillar, calling him onward. It is still some distance away, but God now has a landmark to walk towards. The closer he gets, the more the whispers start to fade.

And then they stop, and the silence resumes.

God has now come into a small area that is illuminated, like it was on the surface where an open cavity lies at the bottom of the void. The beam of light appears to be originating from within it. As he is about to take a step to look down into it, a deep, stern voice stops him in his tracks.

"Why are you here?" asks the voice, echoing all around. God spins and turns in different directions, trying to locate the source.

"You should not have come here," comes the voice again.

"Show yourself!" God commands as his eyes begin to glow.

"You no longer have the right to command me." Evil laughter fills the air. "She's found you, hasn't she?"

God whips around to face the cavity again. "Lucifer?" God's voice cracked, echoing off unseen walls. "Lucifer… is that you? I've come to…"

"I do not care about the reason for which you have come," Lucifer says, cutting God off, his voice still unable to be pinpointed. "A thousand years," Lucifer's voice rasped from the pit. "Imprisoned by those I loved. Tormented by my own mind. And you come here now?" There is little that you can say that would make me want to bend an ear to your words, Father."

God ponders over what Lucifer has just said. He has never once taken the time to think of how Lucifer would be affected by his imprisonment. The realization of this begins to weigh heavily on him. "Lucifer, I..."

"Don't." Lucifer cuts him off again. "Don't you dare try apologizing for things you know nothing about." He takes a brief pause. "These last thousand years have been filled with nothing but pain, anger, torture, and anguish. I have been hurt by every... single... person... that has claimed to have loved me. And I have no need for your apology."

God has now figured out that Lucifer's voice is coming from inside the cavity and starts to inch closer. "Everyone?" he asks calmly. Including Lilith? Has she hurt you as well?"

An orange glow begins to rise from the cavity. "You have no right to utter her name," Lucifer growls.

God starts slowly circling the pit. "So, my assumptions were correct. You are somehow the reason for her new...abilities?"

"Me?" Lucifer's voice cracked into a snarl. "No. You sealed her fate. You murdered our child before her eyes. You obliterated her into nothingness. You planted the seed, Father, and I was only the soil."

"Your weakness to that woman has now brought forth a power of immeasurable limitations."

"My weakness?!" Lucifer yells as the light from within the pit burns brighter. "You were weakened by your own mind from a fear of something that did not exist!"

"YOU KNOW NOTHING OF MY FEARS!!!" God screams as he unleashes his pure light.

"I KNOW ALL TOO WELL, YOUR FEARS!!!"

"YOU THINK YOU KNOW!!! YOU THINK YOU KNOW EVERYTHING!"

"I KNOW THAT THOSE CHILDREN COULD HAVE BROUGHT AN END TO THE DARKNESS!"

"THOSE CHILDREN WERE THE REASON FOR THE DARKNESS!"

Lucifer's voice rose like a storm from the pit."NO, THEY WERE NOT!!! THEY MAY HAVE BEEN NEPHILIM, BUT THEY WERE NOT THOSE NEPHILIM!"

Hearing this changes God's anger to curiosity. "What do you know of the Nephilim?"

Lucifer takes a deep breath and calms himself as well, allowing his anger to dull. "Your Nephilim were treated as kings and worshipped as if they were gods. We could have raised those children differently and trained them. Used them as a weapon to defeat the Darkness. But let us be honest, father, it wasn't fear that drove you to do what you did, it was your pride."

"My pride had nothing to do with that." God replies sternly.

"Did it not? I know you better than any one of my siblings. You are the Creator. You couldn't stand to see something you had nothing to do with. Those children could have been the answer to everything!"

"Those children would have led only to damnation."

"Then I'll be damned for eternity." Lucifer snarls back. "You didn't even allow the slightest thought to cross your mind that you may have been wrong. That there may have been another way. You saw only what those before you had seen and blinded yourself to a path that could have rid us of our enemy. How can a new future be born if we use only the past to build it?"

God falls still, Lucifer's words resonating within him.

"I tried telling Lilith the same thing, but she too, was blinded by her rage and clung only to what had been done to her.... That is why I remain here instead of with her."

The clinking of chains snaps God from his thoughts. He walks over to the edge of the cavity and peers down into it, horrified by what he sees.

Lucifer hung in chains that clinked softly with every breath. His once-mighty frame had withered to a scarred, grey husk, hairless and thin, eyes reduced to two blue sparks in sunken sockets.

God drops to his knees in shame. "My son," he stammers, "what has she done to you?"

Lucifer looks up at him, and they meet eyes. "She has merely carried out your sentence."

Chapter
18

A Mother Scorned

"Lucifer." Lilith whispers, her words echoing multiple times. "Lucifer wake up."

Lucifer's eyes flew open, and a ragged breath escaped his chest. Cold stone pressed against his skin, his own breathing echoing back at him from the dark. He blinked, but the void stayed black. Had he gone blind? He quickly gets to his knees and attempts to stand.

"Aaaauuuggghhh!" he shrieks as he falls back down. It feels like fire is rising from his back.

Again, he attempts to rise to his feet, but again he falls, the cold stone flattening the side of his face. "Where am I?" He tries to recall, but his memory is blank.

"Lucifer," Lilith calls out again

"Lilith?... Are you there?"

But silence is his only answer. The pain that he is in is unimaginable, but slowly he begins crawling on his stomach in the direction of Lilith's voice. The dark devoured all sense of time. Stone scraped beneath his palms as he crawled on and on, his own heartbeat the only sound. Only when his arms trembled from exhaustion did he manage to lift himself onto his knees.

"Come find me," her voice echoes.

Lucifer gets to his feet as his memory starts to recollect. He staggered forward, every step a shamble. Flashes of the Garden tore through his mind, his strike at God, Raphael's fall, chains biting his wrists, each memory lancing his skull with pain until he gasped aloud.

He sees God's arrival to the garden. "Ahhggh."

He sees himself striking his father and throwing Raphael.

"Mmmpphh."

He sees himself in chains and trying to break free. How God forced Michael to kill his son.

"Errraghh."

He sees Michael's face and the remorse that rested on it. He sees Lilith and the fear in her eyes.

"Nnnoo."

God holding her and burning her alive instantaneously.

He falls to his knees and tumbles. He sees the Darkness come over him.

"Satan shall be my name." revolves around his head.

"Then fall." he hears, recalling the moment God tore off his wings.

"EERRGGGAAHHH!!!"

And then he sees the image of the perfect garden, the same image he saw before attacking his father, and a calmness falls over him. He sees the beautiful orange hues of a spring sunset. The vibrant colors of varied species of flowers. The trees with large leaves gently blowing in the wind, as the lush grass does the same. A perfect apple tree with ripe red apples sits in the middle of it all.

"Home," he whispers as he opens his eyes.

He has fallen into a small cavity in the stone. As his eyes adjust, he can see that something nearly invisible lies beside him. He squinted into the void, straining to make out the shape. Then the stone beneath him quivered as a whisper brushed his ear:

"Lucifer."

"Lilith!" he shouts excitedly as he reaches out and grabs the orb. "Lilith, my love, I am so sorry," he says, crying as he clutches the blackened soul.

But Lilith does not respond. He sits up to his knees and holds Lilith's soul in his hands, between his knees.

"Lilith?" he asks softly. "Lilith, are you there?"

But she does not answer him. He starts thinking frantically.

A body… she needed a body. The thought hit him like a jolt, and he scrambled to his feet.

Lucifer quickly sets Lilith's soul down and starts channeling all his energy, groaning as he strains to do so. Slowly but surely, he begins to glow.

"Okay. Good, that's step one." He says as he examines himself. He looks around in search of something that he can use as a starting point, but the area is bare. The only thing he has is himself. He lets out a soft groan, knowing that what he is about to do is going to be highly uncomfortable.

He looks over at the lifeless orb.

"I do this for you." He says before reaching inside of himself, grabbing one of his lower ribs, and snapping it off. Blood drips from his wound as he pulls it out and curses under his breath. Cradling his wound, he summoned what little light still lived within him and began to shape it, breath by breath, like a sculptor working in darkness.

Even though he is producing light, the darkness around him only allows him to see his hands from which the light is flowing. He starts to mold the body from the best of his memory, but he is working all but blindly.

Hours go by as he works to create a vessel for Lilith to the best of his ability. Finally, he reaches a point where he feels that he has completed his task, and he feels all over the body.

The vessel was flawed, its skin uneven, its form imperfect, a mirror of his own fractured state, but it had a voice, a heart, limbs to move. It would be enough. Besides, they won't be able to see anything down here, and she will understand.

He grabs the body and lifts it out of the cavity. Then he reaches down, grabs the orb, and carefully climbs out himself. With the orb in one arm, he stands the empty vessel up with the other.

"Please work," he mutters to himself.

He then holds up Lilith's soul to the chest of the new body. The orb begins to vibrate hard and rips itself free of Lucifer's grip, flying into the vessel.

And then, stillness.

At least for a moment.

A soft thumping starts to fill Lucifer's ears. There would be a single thump, a long pause, and then another thump. Soon, the thumping became more regular and rhythmic.

"A heartbeat!" Lucifer exclaims happily.

He begins to hear the other organs and muscles start to function and come alive, and it wasn't long until Lilith was born again.

Lilith takes her first breath in her new body, then a few more. Her eyes begin to flutter open, and as they do, the darkness parts and gives way to the luster of a moonless night's light. She looks down in disbelief as she admires the body that she now has.

"Lilith! Oh, Lilith, my love, it is so good to see you!" he says with watery eyes.

She sees Lucifer standing before her, a large smile across his face. She cups her mouth and starts to cry at the sight of her lover still alive.

She stumbled into his arms, clutching him with trembling hands. He held her close, both of them collapsing to their knees as a sobbed laugh escaped her lips.

His arms around her bring her the comfort and security she so desperately needed. The warmth of his chest pressed against her cheek provides her with healing energy and a feeling of solace. His head resting atop hers brings her joyful memories of their early days together and the love that they shared.

The love that they lost...

Her tears of joy turn to sobs of sorrow. Memories of what she bore witness to and of what was done to her render her paralyzed. Her body falls limp in Lucifer's grasp, yet still he holds her. She can feel his tears soaking through her hair.

The forbidden lovers mourn the loss of their children and home.

Together they sat in the coldness of the void, crying until they no longer had tears. They then sat in silence for hours as she rested within the comfort of his arms. Her eyes stared off into the distance as she replayed the memory of the knife being shoved into her child.

That was the moment she died.

Her body may have been functioning while God burned her, but her soul was no longer in it. It left when her child was murdered.

Everyone in the garden at that time was focused on what had just happened. No one noticed the tiny orb of light coming out of its vessel and floating away, dulling the higher it got.

It rose through the stratosphere and into the vacuum of space. It traveled beyond the light barrier and into the Darkness where its outer layer was penetrated. The Darkness swept within it, corrupting it down to its very last atom.

And there it remained for a period. It wasn't long before the stars began to lose their energy, and The Darkness was able to rush back into the garden and devoid it of life. The speed at which The Darkness took over caused the orb to crash through the earth and hit the bottom of the pit so hard that a crater was formed.

Slowly Lilith began to come to. She tried to move but couldn't. She then realized that she could not see or feel, only hear, and sense. Panic set in as did the reality that, through no fault of her own, she had been imprisoned.

Frantically, she tried to sense anything that could help her. She strained with all her might, searching for an inkling of something. She didn't know where she was or what had happened, but she prayed that she was not alone.

Then she caught a sense of something familiar.

"What is that?" she asked herself.

She was scanning in all directions so fast that she felt an energy source, but only for a fraction of a second. Quickly she tried locating it again.

"There!"

She had locked in on it. It is far away and very faint, but it is there.

"Lucifer? Lucifer is that you?"

Sadly, she does not get a response even after trying for hours.

For hundreds of years, Lilith had sat alone in the dark calling out to Lucifer with only her memories to keep her company. Few of which were good. That tragic day played out in her mind endlessly turning a once free-flowing spirit into a vengeful one.

But now she is here in Lucifer's arms. But why was she in Lucifer's arms?

Lilith pulls herself up and separates from Lucifer, looking him in the eye as she does so. "How are you here?"

Lucifer adverts his eyes from her as he rubs his head and down to his mouth before looking at her again. "Because I lost."

He shrugs his shoulders, then drops his arms, causing his hands to hit his thighs, making a slapping sound as they do.

"I wasn't strong enough. Not for you. Not for our children. Not even for myself. I thought that I was doing the right thing. And because of my actions, I have caused great pain to all those who have loved me." he says as he reaches out to touch Lilith's face.

THWACK

Lilith strikes Lucifer across the face, knocking him back and off balance. "How dare you cry victim here?" she snarls, her voice becoming deeper.

Lucifer sits up, shock and confusion easily read on his face.

Lilith stares down at him. "You are lucky that I need you," she says and then turns and begins to take in the surrounding area.

Lucifer stands up slowly. "What do you mean?"

Lilith snaps back around to face him. "You promised that you would be there for us." Her voice trembles in sorrow as she speaks. "Yet when the time came, you threw yourself away so easily and without thought. You acted like a wild animal defending its territory instead of the calculating being that you are... That you were."

Tears of fury streaked her cheeks. "You let yourself be bound," she spat. "They toyed with me. They broke me. It led to my death and a level of fear inflicted on me that I cannot describe. And as horrible as that was, it still was nothing compared to the pain I felt when I watched my child die!"

She folds her arms and covers her mouth, turning her head away, trying to snuff her cries. She stands up and walks a short distance away.

Lucifer is speechless. How could he argue with her? Everything that she said was right. He walks over and gently wraps her in a hug. She falls into him, allowing her tears to flow freely. He holds her tight and doesn't say a word; he just lets her cry.

A couple of minutes go by before Lucifer chooses to speak. "I will fix this."

Lilith's crying slows as she looks up at him. "How?" she asks

"After I watched you die, something inside of me broke. More like shattered. I no longer felt the warmth of the light within me. Just a cold, empty nothingness. And then rage set in, and The Darkness followed. I allowed it to enter me, possess me, and in doing so, I became something far more powerful than my father. A devil"

He looks down into Lilith's eyes.

"You should have seen his eyes, he was terrified." He says as he extends Lilith out by her shoulders. "I just need to let the Darkness back in and become that thing again."

A sharp pain enters Lucifer's stomach as a stunned groan of pain forcibly exits his mouth.

He reels back from receiving a monstrous blow to the stomach. He clutches himself and looks to see that it was delivered by Lilith, who is now in the midst of kicking him across the jaw. The blow sends Lucifer spinning through the air and landing just short of the cavity. He confusingly looks at her as she slowly walks towards him.

"I am that thing," she says, an evil grin forming across her lips.

Lucifer attempts to get to his feet, but Lilith pins him down by the throat with her foot. Dark energy begins to swirl around her as her body begins turning into the form that would later take Ralphael's life.

Lucifer is stunned to see that she has been hiding this from him the whole time. "It must be me," he chokes out. "This is my fight."

"You're still wrapped up in your pride." Lilith talks down to him. "You still only see one path. A path that leads nowhere. I have been down here for two hundred years planning this. The Darkness has gifted me with visions beyond my wildest dreams. It has shown me that there are many paths that need to be taken, and you are going to help me get there."

"Then what was all of that before? The happiness to see me? The tears of joy and sorrow?"

"I needed to do that in order to rid myself of it all. To prove to myself that I had but one use for you."

Lucifer struggles to remove Lilith's foot from his throat. "I vowed to unleash Hell upon them!" he frustratedly shouts up at her. "We can do it together!"

She leaned down, pressing her foot harder into his throat, her voice suddenly quiet. "Hell has no fury like that of a mother scorned."

Lucifer's vision begins to fade. His last sight is of Lilith pushing him into the cavity as the Darkness swirls around her.

"You had your chance, and you failed. Now I will take from you what I need, then I will leave you to rot in your prison... My Love."

Chapter
19

A Deal with the Devil

God sat on the cold stone, his fingers tracing shallow grooves as Lucifer's voice, hoarse and thin, recounted the tortures he had endured. Lilith, now wielding the Darkness, had twisted his Light into her army and left him a husk.

"How long did this go on?" God asks

"Nearly eight hundred years," Lucifer rasped, his hands shaking as though the memory alone stole his strength. "She keeps me alive only as a source to fuel her fires."

God rests his head in his hand. "So, there is now a being of free will that is possessed by a corrupted soul, has a body made from the light of an archangel, and is empowered by the Darkness..." he says defeatedly as he drops his hand from his face. "Is this the Hell that you had in mind?"

"Is this the suffering that you had promised me?" Lucifer sneers back.

An awkward silence falls between the two of them.

Lucifer lifted his head, his blue-dotted eyes locking on God. "Why didn't you just kill me," he hissed, "the way you killed the others?"

God tilts his head back and lets out a long sigh. "You have spoken about things that happened before my time. Things that I have never told you. I am assuming that you gained this knowledge when the Darkness took hold of you?" He looks down at Lucifer, who gives him a single nod. "So, then Lilith has this knowledge as well."

He stands up and starts walking around. "When I awoke for the first time, I immediately had to start fighting the battle against the Darkness. As you well know. But before then, I didn't just receive the knowledge of my creators; I also received visions of the future. Visions that I have taken great lengths to avoid. They were not complete visions, just brief flashes of moments in time with no explanations."

He walks back over to look at Lucifer. "In one of these visions," God continued after a pause, "I saw that your death also brings upon my own. If this vision were to be true, to kill you would bring the end to myself."

Lucifer shifts his eyes away from his father's as he absorbs the information he has just received. "So, you've come to rescue me? And in return, what? Ask me for my help?"

"Not rescue you." God slides down into the pit. "I came to free you." He says as he breaks the chain around Lucifer's waist.

"I cannot win this battle without you."

The chains on Lucifer's wrists fall, hitting the ground with heavy thuds.

"Either way, I will lose."

He frees Lucifer's ankles.

"Be it by her hands."

He grabs the chain around Lucifer's neck and looks him in the eye. His grip tightening on the metal as if he could crush the dilemma itself.

"Or yours."

The last chain falls, sending the sound echoing throughout the void.

Lucifer starts rubbing his wrists and rolling his neck before locking eyes with God. A tense stare down ensues.

"The thought of killing you has crossed my mind so many times," Lucifer says coldly. "But the truth is, I couldn't kill you now even if I wanted to. Not just because of my current state but, because Lilith would surely kill me in return if I took the chance of revenge from her."

He climbs out of the pit and looks down at God. "So, you can't kill me, and I can't kill you." He starts walking away. "It appears as though we are deadlocked."

God stepped into Lucifer's path, his voice sharp. 'You're still loyal to her? Even knowing the threat she has become?" The Darkness resides within her, Lucifer and the Darkness will not stop until everything is destroyed!"

"I still love her, Father. Even after everything that she has done to me. I cannot nor will not take part in killing her."

God places a hand on Lucifer's shoulder. "Lucifer, I said nothing of killing her. Help me defeat her and rid this world of the Darkness, and I promise that I will allow you and her to live out the rest of eternity in peace. Somewhere far away where our paths will never intersect again."

Lucifer dropped his gaze, thumb brushing the scar at his wrist. The words came haltingly. 'Promise me,' he said, 'that you will not kill her.'

"I promise," God says as he extends his hand.

Again, Lucifer turns away and thinks heavily about his father's offer. His trust in him is next to nothing but he knows that God would not be here if his intentions were ill. And if there was even the slightest chance that he and Lilith could be together again, he had to take it.

He turned back, eyes shadowed but resolute, and clasped God's hand. A tremor passed through the void. "Then we have a deal.

Chapter
20

The Return Home

Gripping Lucifer's hand, God channels some of his own energy and passes it through to Lucifer. Lucifer looks at God in surprised disbelief as he begins to regain his natural physique. Seeing the look on Lucifer's face, God says, "If we're going to work together, we will need to be able to trust each other." Still holding onto Lucifer's hand.

Lucifer looks at the light flowing into him from God's hand, feeling its warmth running through his veins. He has been deprived of light for so long, yet he now feels as though he was never without it. God's grace is truly amazing. His hair returns to its full volume as his skin turns from grey to light peach. His muscles regain their strength and shape. Even his scars begin to fade.

Lucifer flinched as a tingling built between his shoulders. He yanked his hand free, eyes wide. "No," he said, voice steady but eyes glinting with something like sorrow. "I do not want those returned to me. That life is gone." Looking God in the eyes, he continues. "I appreciate you returning my strength, but those wings are no longer a part of me. You have my trust, but I am not an angel anymore."

God looks at him in slight frustration. "If you are not fully returned to your former glory, you will not make it through the trip home. The Darkness will consu..." He is cut off by Lucifer.

"This is my home," Lucifer says calmly. "Though it may not be what it once was, this will always be my home."

"Lucifer, I struggled to make it here. The path back home..." God pauses to correct himself. "The path back is not an easy one. The moment we leave here, the Darkness will try to devour us and continue trying to do so the entire time, and it is a long journey."

"The Darkness will try to devour you; it will only try to possess me. Which, to be fair, I will need to allow it to do so to fight in our upcoming battle." Lucifer says while shrugging his shoulders and holding his arms up. "My dilemma lies in the fact that once I do allow it in, Lilith will be made aware."

They fell into silence. God stared at the scarred ground, weighing options; Lucifer looked down the corridor of the void in the direction he had fallen into it all those years before. After a few minutes, God looks at Lucifer and says, "We need to get to the surface. I need to make your siblings aware of what is about to transpire so they can be ready. They also may have information as to Lilith's whereabouts."

Lucifer nods in agreement and though somewhat ashamed, allows God to take him by the hand before they begin their ascent to the surface.

When they are about to breach the surface, Lucifer closes his eyes, unsure if he wants to see what it looks like. God notices this and sets him down gently without saying a word. He gives Lucifer the time that he needs and watches his breathing go from short and quick to long and steady.

Finally, Lucifer opened his eyes. Ash coated the ground like frost, and the air hung cold and metallic. Every fiber of him longed to collapse and weep, but he stayed upright, fists trembling. His last memories of the garden were of when it was full of beauty and life. Now all that remains is a blackened and barren landscape.

It used to be full of joyful sounds like the birds chirping and the running stream. He used to feel the warmth of the sun on his skin. Now it was silent and cold, a grim reminder of what had taken place here.

Lucifer glanced at God, staring into the dead horizon. A flicker of anger rose, the same eyes that had condemned him now mourned the loss, but he forced himself to breathe and remember their deal. "Maybe you should start focusing on our way out of here instead of dwelling on the past."

God looks over at him in a "look who's talking" manner. "You are not the only one who lost something that day."

A tense moment is shared between them. Both have thoughts that they wish to put into words, but neither want to initiate the conversation.

Eventually, God looks to the heavens, searching for the home star. The sky is different from when he first arrived here. He soon realizes that they have drifted even further away from the Light.

"Michael," he calls out, but is only met with silence. "Michael, can you hear me?" Again, nothing. "I don't understand," God says aloud. "How have we drifted so far in such a short amount of time?"

"Maybe we should find the location of where you first entered this realm?" Lucifer suggests.

"That would be by the pond," God replies.

Lucifer lets out a sigh. "Of course it would be there." He holds out his arm and gestures in the direction of the pond. "That would be this way," he says and begins walking.

"It would be much faster if I flew you to it."

"I figured that there would be two times that I would have to allow you to lift me up. Once out of the pit and once off the surface. I do not have the tolerance for a third." He turns and looks God in the eyes. "We walk."

Frustrated, God contemplates insisting but knows that it will fall on deaf ears. So, he too, begins walking.

They walk for hours together, but alone in their own thoughts. The crack in the earth narrows as time passes, giving them the satisfaction of knowing that they will reach the pond soon. But, without warning, Lucifer stops abruptly and uses his hand to stop God as well.

Sensing something is wrong, God whispers. "What is it?"

"I'm not sure," Lucifer whispers back. "For a moment I thought I heard something."

The two remain silent as they strain to hear whatever it was that caused Lucifer to stop. However, after a minute of hearing nothing further, they look at each other and agree to continue on.

"What do you think you heard?" God asks

"I'm not sure. It was probably just the intense silence playing tricks on my mind."

Or at least that's what he tells God.

Yet in his bones, he was sure that it had been a child's cry. He pressed his heel into the dirt, leaving a mark only he would understand, and kept walking without a word.

A few hours later, they reach their destination. As Lucifer walks around and examines the remains, God looks into the abyss in the direction that he came from.

"Michael? Michael, can you hear me?"

Still nothing.

"Michael, Uriel, Gabriel? Are any of you there?" he calls out again.

Again, he hears no response. He lets out a sigh and continues scanning the stars, trying to find home. But then.

"Father? Father, is that really you?" Michael responds hesitantly.

"Yes, my child!" God responds in relief. "It is I."

"Father, we thought you were gone."

"I am sorry. I will explain everything once we have returned. Are you all safe?"

There is a brief pause before Michael responds.

"We? So, you've found him? You've found Lucifer?"

God notices that Michael's voice is a bit different but sets it aside. "I have found him. Again, I will explain everything once we return. But Michael, I must warn you, we are not certain on what is going to happen on our journey back, so be prepared for anything."

"Understood. We are waiting."

God turns and extends his hand out to Lucifer. Lucifer takes one last look around the garden. "I will not forget," he says to himself. Then he walks over and takes God's hand.

God drew a deep breath and let his Light swell, white radiance spilling from his skin until the air vibrated. He gripped Lucifer's hand tighter. 'Are you ready?' he asks.

"As I'll ever be," Lucifer responds as he stares into The Darkness.

God, still with a firm grip on Lucifer's hand, leaps into the awaiting Darkness. Just as before, he is immediately met by a storm, relentlessly trying to tear him apart. But it is much more difficult now. Before he was able to focus only on himself and use all his strength to weather the storm. Now, he has Lucifer that he needs to pull along and protect.

God pushes his boundaries and makes himself glow even brighter, trying to create a pocket of safety. Chaos ensues, and God is quickly becoming aware that this may be a task too difficult to bear. "There is no other way," he tells himself, trying to remain encouraged. He can still feel Lucifer in his hand, but cannot take away his focus to check on him.

Lucifer senses his father's struggle, so he reaches out telepathically. "We are not going to make it this way. Let me help you."

"No," God says sternly. "We cannot risk her finding you."

"If I do not help, there will not be a 'we' for her to find." Lucifer snaps back.

God growls, knowing Lucifer is right. "Michael!" he calls out. "Be ready to fight." He then looks down at Lucifer and heavily hesitates.

Lucifer meets his gaze and understands his hesitation. "If we're going to work together, we will need to be able to trust each other," he quotes God's words.

"Let it within you, but do not let it consume you," God tells him. Lucifer gives him a single nod, and against his better judgment, God releases Lucifer's hand and watches as he fades into the Darkness. God has no choice but to leave him and press on.

Power surges through Lucifer's veins as he allows the Darkness within him. It tries to snuff out his Light and he can feel it tugging away at his mind, begging him to let it take over. Lucifer is tempted to let it do so. To allow it to consume him and make him the devil he was before.

Images flashed: tearing his father apart, crushing the skull that once blessed him. The Darkness hissed its promises. Lucifer's fingers curled as if already holding the fragments.

Lucifer's eyes roll back into his skull from the euphoria that he is feeling.

The power feels so good.

"No!" he says to himself, snapping back to reality. He fights off those thoughts knowing that if he allows that to happen, he and Lilith will never know peace.

He battles the darkness within his own mind and, in turn, begins to control the Darkness that was now within his body. After a moment, his internal struggle is over, and he has won. He looks at his hands and body and sees that they have turned black. Then he reaches out, pulls a strand of the Darkness, and rolls it around his hand like a snake slithering between his fingers. "Not yet," he whispers to himself.

Lucifer peers in the direction that God was headed. He sees the storm that has engulfed God, barely allowing any of God's light to shine through. He grabs onto the Darkness and uses it to propel himself towards his father at blinding speed.

Lucifer cut a swath through the storm, yanking the Darkness aside as though parting a black sea. In its wake, a corridor of stillness formed for God to move through. God turns, looking to see what has caused this, and Lucifer sees his eyes widen at the shock of it all.

"We must hurry," Lucifer said, sweat beading on his brow. Shadows writhed along his arms, pulsing as though alive. "The longer I hold this form, the easier it is for her to sense me. If she hasn't already."

Lucifer's voice has remained the same. Hearing this causes God to smile. "I'm glad that it's still you in there," he says.

"Hmph," Lucifer replies with a slight grin. "Lead on."

They continue their travel through space. As glimpses of the Light Barrier begin to come into view, God notices Lucifer look away like something caught his attention. "What is it?" he asks.

"She knows that we're here," Lucifer says grimly.

"How do you know?"

He looks at God. "Because if I can sense her, she can sense me."

God looks around in search of any signs of Lilith, but it is nearly impossible to see anything past the pocket of light that Lucifer has given them. "Is she close?"

"I don't think so. But she will be once she figures out what's happening."

Suddenly they pierce the veil of the Light Barrier causing Lucifer to scream out in pain and stop moving. God notices that Lucifer is no longer beside him and turns to see that he is twisted in agony. "What's wrong?!" God yells back at him, but Lucifer is unable to speak. God hurriedly flies back over to Lucifer and places a hand on him. This causes Lucifer to scream even more.

A shrill and hollow scream pierces through the veil.

God looks up and sees The Darkness parting, giving way to Lilith. She comes to a stop right at the edge of the Light Barrier. She looks at Lucifer's twisted body, then to God and the hand he has on Lucifer.

Seeing the pattern in which Lilith has seen everything, God looks at his own hand resting on Lucifer, then back to Lilith. Putting it all together, he realizes what this must look like. This causes God to say something very uncharacteristic of him.

"Ah Fuck."

Lilith's eyes turn black, and her body tenses. She throws her arms back and unveils her legion behind her. It is a mix of steadfast corrupted angels surrounded by the gnawing and snapping of the shadow creatures.

Two of the corrupted angels stand beside Lilith. They look much different than the others, but God has no time to dwell on it. Frantically, he pulls at Lucifer, trying to get him closer to Sanctuarium. "Lucifer, you need to release the Darkness, and you need to do it now!"

Lilith screams again, causing God to look back at her. Without care for any members of her Dark Army, she sends them stampeding from the Darkness and into the Light. The entire Dark Army runs past her and the other two, charging at God.

Panic surges through God's veins. He knows that he cannot fight them all on his own for any period of time longer than a minute, if even that. But he also knows that he cannot leave Lucifer behind. He needs to make up his mind quickly.

"So be it," he says as he places himself between Lucifer and the Dark Army. He closes his eyes and takes a large deep breath. Then he opens them and braces himself for the onslaught that was charging him.

Right before Lilith's forces reach him, a blinding flash of light stops them in their tracks and causes them to reel back. God turns around and sees Michael, Uriel, and Gabriel in front of a large, unprecedented army of angels.

God's eyes widen in disbelief. The army was outfitted with armor harder than any other metal and was golden in color. They carried long rectangular shields and spears made of hard light. They stood shoulder to shoulder in rows of a hundred divided into garrisons stretching back farther than God could see from where he currently was.

"How?" he asks. But Michael ignores that question as he stares down Lilith.

"Get the Darkness out of Lucifer," Michael commands without breaking eye contact. "We can hold them off, but we will not win here."

God looks down at Lucifer. "I'm sorry," he whispers. He then begins to burn the Darkness by forcing his Light through Lucifer, like expelling venom from his veins, again causing Lucifer to cry out in pain.

Lilith hears this. "Bring him to me!" she screams, causing the Dark Army to resume their attack.

God blazed brighter, forcing the Darkness out until it shredded into smoke. Lucifer went slack in his arms. Without another glance at Lilith, God launched toward the Light, his own strength fraying as Michael's army covered their retreat.

Soon they are within the safety of the Light and Michael catches up to God. He looks at Lucifer's unconscious body in God's arms. God sees Michael looking at Lucifer, but notices that Michael has changed. He has aged slightly.

"Come, Father." Michael's voice snaps God from his thoughts. "A lot has changed since you left. It has been a long time, and we have much to discuss."

Chapter
21

Preparation Part i

Uriel and Gabriel stand in the entryway of Sanctuarium watching Michael pace back and forth in front of the entry door. "You're going to wear a hole in that floor," Gabriel says sarcastically. Michael shoots a glance at him but continues pacing. "Seriously, Michael, c'mon, he's going to understand."

"That is not what I am concerned about." Michael snaps back. He has come to a standstill now. "My concern is that our greatest threat is lying unbound and unconscious in the very heart of our sanctuary, inside the one barrier that keeps us alive," he says as he glares at Gabriel. "And if you're not aware, that lies within the boundary of the only thing keeping us all alive!"

"I am quite aware, Michael, but you have placed our best guards there. And beyond that, do you really think Father would risk bringing Lucifer here if he thought that it would damage us?"

"I am pleased that our father is alive. However, I have reservations about his intentions. He has spent the last few decades beyond the Light Barrier and within the limits of The Darkness. We cannot yet be sure that his mind has not been altered."

The massive doors swung open, spilling a shaft of light across the hall. God stepped inside and paused, stunned. His home had become a fortress of light, alive with murmurs and movement. What was once just an empty ball of light with a floor and a few walls, has now been made larger to hold the vast numbers of the Angelic Army.

The original concept has been kept with the walls and floors being made of hard light, but it is a thousand times larger than before and is now two levels. It is precisely forty-four hundred feet wide, seventy-two hundred feet long, and fifty feet high. The exterior walls are still a bright white light that gives the illusion that they are moving as the light revolves around within them. However, the interior walls have been dimmed so that it is easier to see inside.

In the center of the front wall are two large doors that open inward, and instead of walking into the Main Hall that held the Great Table, God has now walked into the Great Hall that is exceptionally long with high, arched ceilings. It is the only area that has no second floor.

There are seven doors on each side of the Great Hall that are spaced evenly throughout the length of the room. These doors lead to other halls that provide resting quarters, branching from them with staircases at the ends that lead to the second floor. The second floors match the layout of the first.

At the far end of the Great Hall is a staircase that is wide at the bottom and narrows as it goes up. The stairs rise twenty-five feet, and at the top is a door that leads to the original Main Hall, the resting quarters of the four archangels, and God's workstation.

"You've been busy," God says, still taking it all in.

"So have you," Michael replies, half irritated.

God turns to look at Michael. The scar on the left side of his face remains prominent, but God now is sure that Michael has aged. He has creases in the skin around his eyes and mouth, and his brow line is furled. He has a larger beard but still wears his hair in locks.

Michael sees God examining him and begins leading the four of them down the Great Hall. They walk in silence until they climb the stairs and enter the privacy of the Main Hall.

They all choose a side and stand next to the Great Table. Michael is at the far side of the table with Uriel to his left and Gabriel to his right. God stands at the end closest to the entry. He looks over at Uriel and Gabriel and notices that they too, have aged. He lets out a deep sigh before asking a dreaded question.

"How long have I been gone?"

Uriel and Gabriel look at each other with their eyebrows raised before looking at Michael to answer, causing God to also look at him.

Michael stood rigid at the far side of the table, arms folded across his chest, head tilted slightly, locking his eye on God's, the posture of a commander addressing an equal, not a subordinate. It is almost like he is disregarding God's authority.

"How long have I been gone, Michael?" God asks again.

"Forty years," Michael replies gruffly.

"Forty years?!" God's hands gripped the edge of the table as his light faltered for a heartbeat. "Impossible. I was gone three, maybe four days." He looks at the other two archangels for confirmation, but their faces show that Michael is telling the truth.

"You were so quick to act on your plan that you never gave consideration to all of the factors of it," Michael says sternly. "You left us giving little regard as to what could happen in your absence."

"Michael, this does not make any sense," God says as he looks down at the table. "How much time passed from the time that I left until I reached the Forsaken Garden?"

"Two days." God looks up at him as he says this. "Two days and then nothing for forty years."

God lowers his head in thought. "I do not understand," he says while shaking his head.

Michael sighs and relaxes his body while placing his hands on the table to lean on it. He can tell by his father's expression that he genuinely did not know. "What happened down there?" he asks gently.

"After I reached the bottom of the void, I started walking in the only direction that I could. I began hearing whispers echoing, but the voices were unfamiliar. I kept walking for what seemed like hours to me until I came across an opening with a small crater resting in the middle. As I got closer, a remarkably familiar voice spoke to me." He pauses and looks up. "It was Lucifer."

God continues. "He explained to me that he woke up hearing whispers as well that led him to the same spot and there he found Lilith's soul. He constructed a body for her and then revived her, thinking that they would start anew together. However, that dream was short-lived."

Michael, Uriel, and Gabriel all stare at God in anticipation.

"Lucifer soon found out that Lilith had been toying with him. Her soul had already been consumed and revived by the Darkness; she just needed a body. And Lucifer delivered. After having her fun, she restrained Lucifer as we had and used him to strengthen herself and her army.

She then left him there to rot.

When I found him, he was barely anything at all. A mere fragment of who he once was."

A quiet falls over the room as the three archangels absorb the information that their father has just given them. They weren't sure what God's explanation was going to be, but they definitely were not expecting it to be that.

"She merely carried out my sentence," is what he told me," God says somberly. "The only explanation that I can come up with for the discrepancy in time is that it must have moved differently in the void, although I still am uncertain as to how."

The four of them stare down at the table without saying a word as they try to figure out why time has moved differently between the two parties. Michael is looking at the wood grain and notices how the closer they are to the center the denser they become but become farther apart the farther away they are from the center.

He runs his finger over the table's wood grain, watching the rings narrow at the center. "Time here must move like a tree grows," he said. "Strongest at its core, weaker and faster as it radiates outward."

He looks over to God.

"Since you are the source of all creation, time flows as intended around you, no matter where you are."

"And moves faster where I am not." God finishes Michael's thought, now understanding.

Gabriel chimes in with his own thought. "So, if you say that you were gone for four days, then that would mean that in the Forsaken Garden, time would move at a ratio of ten to one. One year here would be ten years there.... Has Lucifer really been imprisoned for ten thousand years?"

Again, they all go quiet as the realization sets in. It is true that Lucifer would not have felt that he was imprisoned that long, but they all know now that he was, and that thought sickens them.

"How did you convince Lucifer to come back with you?" Uriel asks after a few minutes in an attempt to change the subject.

God looks at her and then to Michael, knowing that he is not going to be fond of his answer.

"I promised him that if he helped defeat Lilith and rid her of the Darkness, then he can take her to live in peace for the rest of their days, far away and left alone."

Upon hearing this, Gabriel covers his face, and Uriel hangs her head. They know how this is going to go.

"You did WHAT?!" Michael's voice cracked like thunder as light sparked across his shoulders, making Uriel flinch. "I am going to assume that your time in the void clouded your judgement because there is no way that in your right mind, you would have made that promise."

"My judgment was not clouded, and I will remind you of your position here boy," God says, also growing angry.

"You ran off on your little adventure, leaving me to handle everything for the last four decades, and you want to remind me of my position?!" Michael leans in. "You abandoned your position and left it all to me!"

God ignites his eyes in fury.

"I did what was necessary!"

"No, you did not!" Michael steps in while starting to glow. "If you would have been patient, you would have seen that there was another option. The option that led us to where we are today! But as you always do, you look to the past for answers instead of the present."

God's eyes slowly dull as Michael's words resonate within him. He takes into consideration that, to him, it has been less than a week since they have all spoken, but they have had to grow accustomed to his absence and were forced to move on. Despite him feeling disrespected, he was proud of how they had all grown and handled the situation and decided that anger is not served best here.

"Forgive me," God says to all of them. "Please believe that if I had known the outcome would have been this, I never would have left you all."

Uriel's eyes glistened as she stepped forward. She pressed her face into God's chest, inhaling the faint scent of ozone that clung to him. "I've missed you so much," she whispered through a tremor in her voice.

God rests his head on top of hers and squeezes her tightly. "I am so sorry, my dear child." He then looks over at Gabriel, who meets his gaze.

Gabriel tries to resist but can't and quickly walks over to hug his father as well. "I've missed you as well," he says as God opens his arms for him to join Uriel.

Michael watched the embrace from the doorway, jaw clenched. It should have been a comfort, yet the sight of it stirred old wounds, decades of leadership, grief, and waiting pressed like a weight against his chest., He was still angry at his father for what he had done and the promise that he had made to Lucifer.

God looks up and sees Michael walking over. A smile forms on his face as Michael gets closer, but it fades when he realizes that he has not come to join the embrace. Instead, Michael walks right by them and exits the room.

"He'll come around," Gabriel says after noticing God's disappointment. "Your absence weighed on him the most; he mourned your loss for ages.

The three of them let go of one another and take a step back, giving each other some room.

"It's true," Uriel says. "He locked himself away for days. Then, out of nowhere, he came out and told us that he was going to go find you. We tried to stop him, but it was to no avail. Our pleas were ignored."

"What did he do?" God asks concerningly.

"He attempted to breach the veil," answers Gabriel. "He got farther than I thought he would but had to quickly return. His anger wasn't a strong enough source to get him through the journey.

Then he thought that Lilith might have some answers, so he challenged her to a one-on-one fight and got his backside handed to him. This was all within the first two weeks after your disappearance. After that, he locked himself away again, except this time he made use of your workstation."

"What was he doing?"

Uriel and Gabriel look at each other. Gabriel is about to say something, but Uriel quickly interjects.

"That may be a question best answered by Michael, Father."

"Then I guess I should go and find him," God says, knowing exactly where to go.

A few minutes later, he arrives back at the infirmary where he finds Michael standing next to an unconscious Lucifer lying on a bed. His back is to God, but he knows he is there. God walks around to the other side of the bed and also looks down at Lucifer.

They stand in silence for a while before God speaks.

"You've done well by them. Uriel and Gabriel, I mean." Michael continues to ignore him. "You've done well by me, too." Michael shoots him a glance, then goes back to looking at Lucifer. "They told me that you tried to find me, and when that failed, you challenged Lilith?"

Still, he is ignored.

"Michael, talk to me. Please."

"What is it exactly that you are looking for me to say? Hmm? I am happy to see you Father, truly. But I cannot set aside the time that has passed since we last spoke. Yes, you may have fulfilled your promise of return, but that was decades ago.

We were in shambles. Raphael had just been slain, and our forces were severely reduced. We clung to the hope of your quick return, but our waiting went from days to weeks to years while our enemy grew stronger and nearer.

I had to abandon the hope of your return and seek out other ways to regain our strength, or we would have been destroyed. Then you return after forty years and expect it all to go back to the way it was?"

Michael stops and shakes his head.

"We are too far past that to return, Father," he says while finally looking at God.

"Michael, I did not know."

"No. You did not listen."

God looks down at Lucifer again. He knows that Michael has a point to an extent, but also realizes that Michael is not currently open to his words, so he decides to drop it.

"How did you accomplish all this?" God says as he motions around. "When I left, this place was little more than a safe haven. Now you have an entire fully equipped army, and what you turned Sanctuarium into is absolutely amazing."

"Not here," Michael says sternly. "Not in front of him." Then he turns and walks out the door. God notices his concern and follows him. When they are a safe distance away and Michael is certain that no one else is around, he motions for God to come close.

"I found a way to harness a new source of energy," he whispers to God.

"A new source of energy?" God questions. "How?"

"I collected resources that had been recovered from various sources and combined them. In doing so, I created a power that I can charge up and use when needed. However, it is fickle, and if I overcharge it in the slightest, it becomes unstable, and I must put the core into a state of dormancy until it cools down and stabilizes itself. It's still a work in progress, but I have it secure enough to use."

"Show it to me."

"Now isn't the time."

"Why is that?"

"Because of who lies behind that door," Michael says as he points to the room they had just exited. "I will not risk him knowing about it."

God looks down in thought. It is obvious that this new energy source is capable of remarkable things; he saw it with his own eyes. Even though he still has many questions, he decides to tuck them away for now. Michael has done well in his absence, and he should not upset the order of things, especially with what is to come.

"I am proud of you, Michael," God says as he puts a hand on his son's shoulder. "If I were in your position, I would share the same cautions."

Michael reached out and clasped his father's shoulder. For a heartbeat the soldier's hardness left his face, replaced by the son he had once been. He squeezed gently and let out a quiet breath. 'I've missed you, Father.'

They then pull each other in for a quick yet meaningful hug before letting go.

"We have a war to prepare for," Michael says. "Do you truly believe that he will help us?"

"If I am being honest with myself, I have my reservations as well. But he loves her, of that I am certain. He could have stayed behind, attacked me, or called out to her, but he did none of those things. He could have very easily killed me in our journey through The Darkness, but in truth, he is the only reason that I made it back. I've found myself questioning if this could have all been avoided if we had just left them alone in the Garden."

"What is done, is done. There is no going back."

God nods in agreement to Michael's statement, then asks, "Are our forces strong enough to defeat hers?"

"They are strong enough to hold their own against the shadow creatures and the corrupted lesser angels. But as for Lilith and her two minions, they stand no chance."

"Her minions? The two that stood beside her?"

"Yes, Caliban and Cronan. They were once members of my order and acted as generals. They had knowledge of our strategies and tactics, which made them extremely valuable to her. I cannot fathom the horrors that must have been inflicted on them, for they would not have gone easily. But this is no place to discuss war plans, Father. Let us return to the Main Hall," he says, and the two of them begin their return, leaving Lucifer in the hands of the guards.

Gabriel and Uriel are awaiting them when God and Michael return. They are pleased to see that their father and older brother appear to have settled their dispute.

"Father and I have come to an understanding of each other's points of view," Michael says as they resume their positions around the table. "Now it is time for us to discuss our strategy of defeating Lilith. Gabriel, what do your scouting reports show?"

Gabriel lays a large map down on the table. On it, it shows Sanctuarium located within the far-right section of the map, with Gabriel's Garden a short distance away to the right. It depicts the location of several stars that orbit Sanctuarium as well as the boundaries of the Light Barrier. Unfortunately, this area only takes up about a quarter of the entire map.

The rest of the map is shaded using hash marks that provide the span of The Darkness that lies beyond them. Within this dark area are pinpointed areas where Lilith and her army are believed to be stationed. Gabriel points at the locations as he begins to talk.

"Our scouts have seen substantial amounts of activity here, here, and here. They have seen Caliban and Cronan at these two locations, but we have no reports of Lilith's whereabouts since you returned."

"No sightings at all?" Michaels asks.

"Not a single one."

"That is highly unusual," chimes in Uriel.

"What about you?" Michael asks her. "Where are our troops positioned?"

Uriel grabs a couple of round golden markers and places five of them around Sanctuarium. "We have five garrisons guarding our perimeter." She then places seven markers in a line behind the Light Barrier. "These garrisons act as our primary defense." Finally, she places the remaining ten markers around Gabriel's Garden. "These are the strongest of our forces that protect the Garden. Should they be needed, one garrison will remain at the Garden for continued protection while the rest join the front line."

"How many angels do we now have?" God asks.

"Seven hundred thousand," replies Michael, causing God's eyebrows to raise in surprise.

"And how many does Lilith's army contain?"

"According to our most recent scouting reports, we estimate roughly twice as many as we do," Gabriel responds. "However, as long as we follow our plan, our angels will be able to handle the hounds," he turns to God, "the shadow creatures, with relative ease. The lesser angels will be a more difficult enemy, but their numbers are limited."

"Our toughest battle will be against Caliban and Cronan," Michael says. "With them being first-generation lesser angels and with the power of The Darkness coursing through them, their strength is now equal to the three of ours. They will keep us busy."

"So that leaves Lucifer and I to deal with Lilith then."

Michael nods his head. "She is much stronger now than she was before you left. She has become the embodiment of The Darkness and nearly immune to light. It will not be an easy task to take her out."

"We are not taking her out," comes a voice from behind them.

The group turns around to see Lucifer standing in the doorway. Gabriel and Uriel's jaws open slightly out of shock and a little fear as Michael poises himself and stares down his brother, his muscles tensing.

Lucifer stares back at Michael, unwavering. A tense moment passes before God steps in between them.

"I will remind the two of you that we are here to work together."

"He should not be here," Michael growls, not breaking eye contact with Lucifer.

"We need him."

A wave of raw emotions fills Michael's thoughts, both good and bad. For the first time in decades, Michael is unsure as to how to react to a situation, for none have been such as this. Before him stands the greatest threat to their existence, but at the same time, it is also the brother who taught him the strength and knowledge to be who he now is.

His instincts tell him that he should end Lucifer here and now, but his heart has gone back to that day. The day that he stood idly by as his brother lost everything, and he, himself, lost his mentor.

But things are different now. Michael had learned long ago that even though Lucifer was blinded by love, he was still responsible for the position that they are in now. The position that found themselves in need of a devil.

He brushes past God and gets close to Lucifer's face. "You are only here because our father believes it necessary." He points back at God. "For reasons I don't fully understand, he trusts you. My trust only stems from his." He lowers his hand and leans in even closer. "Step out of line in the slightest and you will wish that he had not pulled you from that pit."

Lucifer stares coldly at Michael. He too, had conflicted feelings about seeing his siblings. His anger had passed for the most part during his imprisonment, but he had not forgotten how they had treated him in the Garden.

However, he was not prepared to see how much Michael had grown. Not only physically, but his mind had matured to a state where Lucifer almost felt that Michael was the older brother now.

He reminds himself as to why he is here, briefly looking at God before returning to Michael. "You'd better keep an eye on me then," he says as he pushes past him and walks over to the table.

Once he is there, he acknowledges Gabriel and Uriel with a nod. He then looks around as though he is searching for something, confusion furls his brow. "Where is Raphael?"

A saddened silence falls over the room. Lucifer senses everyone's discomfort, picking up on their bodily cues. "He is gone then?" His breath caught. For a fleeting moment, he hoped he was wrong.

Michael walks behind Lucifer and back to his place at the table. "It was by Lilith's hand," he says coldly as he stares his brother down.

Lucifer's eyes drop. Part of him was saddened by this news. Though they had their differences, he and Raphael had shared many fond memories together. But then he remembers what had taken place the last time they had seen each other, and his sorrows fade.

God comes over and places Himself next to Lucifer. He gives Michael a "calm yourself" look before turning to Lucifer and saying; "This is one of the many reasons why we must all work together to bring an end to this conflict. So that no more meaningless deaths need to occur." He directs Lucifer's gaze to the map. "What do you see?"

Lucifer regains his focus on the task at hand. "If your reports are correct and Lilith has not been seen, then I would be tempted to believe that she has gone back to see how you and I came to be within each other's company."

"How certain of this are you?"

"As certain as she would need to be that I was indeed gone."

Lucifer looks up and makes eye contact with everyone individually before resting his gaze on Michael.

"If I know her as well as I think I do, her first thought after finding us would be thinking that you all were attempting to trick her. But the quick retreat would have planted a seed of doubt in her mind that would grow until she needed to know for sure."

"Then we need to attack now before she returns," God says quickly.

"No," Michael says sternly

All eyes now rest on him.

"What do you mean, no?" asks a slightly irritated God.

"Do you not find it suspicious at all that the one who once tried to murder us is now telling us to go into battle without knowing for certain where Lilith is? How do we know that they have not communicated in some way and planned some sort of trap?"

"No one wants this war over more than I do, Michael," says Lucifer sadly. "You all have lost only time. I have lost everything. My family, my grace, my children, my home, and my love. Most of which I have lost forever. There is a void inside me that can never be whole."

He tries to hide the water forming in his eyes.

"But Lilith is alive and if we can rid her of The Darkness then I have a chance to get a part of that life back." Again, he looks directly at Michael. "That is why I am here, and despite what you may think, deceiving you would only hurt me."

Michael feels that Lucifer is being truthful but still he hesitates.

"Michael, we do not have time for this. If Lucifer is correct, then we could wound them significantly before she returns." God says as he walks over. "Give the order to attack or I will."

"They are loyal to me; they will not listen to you. They don't even know who you are!"

"Then you must tell them to obey me," God says sternly.

"Father, it has been forty years since you left and much has changed. Most of these angels know you only as a rumor. They have never even seen you, but they have fought Lilith and The Darkness, they know that threat to be true. They also have heard the stories of Lucifer and what he has caused. Now here you stand telling me that your plan is to tell them to stand behind their most dangerous enemy?" He shakes his head. "It will not work."

God takes a step back, realizing that Michael speaks truthfully. In turn, however, Michael walks over to him and speaks softly.

"In all of your wisdom and knowledge, do you truly believe this to be the only way?" he asks as a son to a father.

"No," God replies in the same manner. "But it is the only way that we will win."

Michael looks over at Lucifer, then over to Uriel and Gabriel, his two closest and most trusted allies. They both give him a nod, telling him that they are with him. He looks back at Lucifer who also gives him a nod before coming back to God.

God places a hand on Michael's shoulder. "I understand your hesitation. War is ugly and wrought with death, and it is no easy task for a leader to send others to fight his battles."

He lowers himself to be at eye level with Michael. "It is your call."

Michael inhales deeply and breathes out slowly. If only he had more time, things could play out differently and without as much risk. But he has his back against a wall and must do what needs to be done.

He looks over his shoulder to Gabriel. Michael straightened and let his voice carry through the hall. "Call the commanders. Ready the ranks. The war begins." Around them, the hall came alive with the low thunder of angels moving into formation.

Preparation Part ii

The Great Hall is filled with murmurs and chatter among the twenty-two garrison leaders of the Angelic Army. Rumors of God's return had spread through the ranks, and they all were eagerly anticipating the validity of said rumors. There were also rumors that the Fallen One had accompanied God in his return.

Among the twenty-two commanders, only four of them had ever witnessed God in the flesh. Their names were Gamaliel, Cassiel, Raguel, and Sariel, and they are the only surviving members of The Order of Michael. This also makes them the last of the first generation of lesser angels.

Sariel and Raguel are both male, and Gamaliel and Cassiel are both females. They all bore the same traits as the other lesser angels, being smaller in size than the Archangels. Their bodies are made from pale yellow light that resonates under their armor with white eyes that change size as needed or based on whatever emotions they are feeling.

They were there when Lilith attacked and killed Raphael and bore firsthand witness to the power that Lilith held. The other eighteen commanders had fought Lilith's forces but never Lilith head-on as these four had. They knew God to be true and had watched him fearlessly cross into the Darkness to confront Lilith, but also held onto the memory of leaving their brothers and sisters behind.

All these things kept them fiercely loyal to God and his cause. They were loyal to Michael as well and acknowledged him as their leader during God's absence. Michael favored these four and held them with profound respect. He trusted them more than any other lesser angels, and they, in turn, showed the same back to him. Because of this, they were the only ones who stood quiet as the others gossiped behind them.

The opening of the Main Hall door creates a quiet throughout the Great Hall as they all turn to see Michael standing before them atop the stairs. He looks out over them all as they fall into order before he makes individual eye contact with the original four then he begins speaking.

"My brothers and sisters, thank you for your patience and for gathering so quickly. As you all know, we have been in a deadlocked war against Lilith and The Darkness. Actively, we have sought solution after solution, and none have put us any closer to ending this war."

He pauses as he tries to convince his mind to say what must be said, still unsure of it himself.

"Few of us in this room have ever seen our creator; most of you believe him only to be myth. But I can tell you with certainty that he is real, and he has indeed returned."

Cheers break out across the room. Smiles are seen and laughter is heard as they all rejoice.

"But he has not returned alone," Michael says over the noise, causing everyone to fall silent.

"We have exhausted all other options that are currently available to us, and our father believes that the one that he has brought with him will enable us to end this war once and for all."

Noticing his struggle, Gamaliel calls out.

"Speak plainly Michael, we can all handle it."

Michael relaxes his shoulders slightly as he looks at Gamaliel in a thankful manner. He then looks back over the crowd as he says,

"God has brought back Lucifer the Fallen."

Gasps and whispers begin to fill the air. Someone within the crowd calls out, "The Fallen One?" Another shouts, "Has he gone mad?"

Cassiel turns around and yells, "QUIET EVERYONE! QUIET! Allow him to finish speaking."

Again, the room falls still.

Michael gives Cassiel a nod of appreciation before speaking again.

"If I am being truthful, I am not certain of this plan either. I have never lied to, nor have I ever led any of you astray, and I will not start today. So, I ask of you, all of you, to lend me your trust again to lead you into this battle. I ask you to have trust in yourselves, trust in each other, and trust in me that I will not set you down a path of demise.

In truth, my father could have easily come out here instead of me and commanded you all to follow without question. Instead, he recognized the change that has happened in his absence and gave me the respect I deserved, as well as the respect you all deserved, to have me speak to you first."

Michael does his best to make eye contact with each of them before he finishes speaking.

"Now it is my turn to give my father the respect that he deserves and allow him to regain command of our forces."

Michael turns to the entryway of the Main Hall and kneels

"Father, my army is yours."

God walks through the door.

Immediately, Gamaliel, Cassiel, Raguel, and Sariel kneel and bow their heads. The others stare in awe at the sight before them. God opens his arms, and the warmth of his grace instantly expels all doubts of his existence from their minds, causing the rest of them to kneel before him.

Uriel and Gabriel have also entered the room, standing behind God. Michael gets up and stands between them as God addresses the commanders.

"My children," he says warmly. "First, I would like to apologize to you all for the length of my absence, it was not intended to be that long. I realize that I have lost a great deal of time with you all, and I thank Michael, Gabriel, and Uriel for stepping up and building everything that is before you." He says as he turns back to look at the three of them.

"Regretfully, we do not have much time," God says, addressing the room again. "We believe that our enemy is in a state of vulnerability and must act quickly. I ask of you all to rally your troops and prepare to launch an assault while the time is right."

"Is it true?" someone in the crowd shouts out. "Have you brought the Fallen One with you?"

"It is true," God replies, causing chatter. "Our enemy has the advantage of being able to fight within both the light and the dark. As soon as they are beaten back, they are able to regroup and rebuild, causing a never-ending cycle. To break this cycle, we needed someone on our side who could fight in the dark. An agreement has been reached between him and I, and he is solely my responsibility."

He pauses for a moment, allowing them to soak in what he is saying before continuing.

"You all are to follow Michael's orders and leave Lucifer as my burden to bear. While you all focus on the Dark Army and its leaders, he and I will find and subdue Lilith, bringing an end to this war once and for all!"

God scans over the crowd as moral starts to heighten.

"I am asking you all to have faith in me and in our cause. Let us rid this world of The Darkness and bring forth peace everlasting!"

Cheers break out as God turns to Michael and the others.

"You have command of our forces. Lucifer and I will join you when the time is right."

"Understood."

"Michael."

"Yes, father?"

"Be careful out there," God says as he walks away.

Michael turns to Uriel and Gabriel. They do not share a word because their words would be empty. But there is no need for words when a trust like theirs is instilled.

Michael then turns to Gamaliel, Cassiel, Raguel, and Sariel, who also say nothing. They have remained stoic in the rally, and Michael can see in their faces that they share his concern, but their loyalty forever lies with the cause. He motions for them to come up and join him and his siblings.

Michael leaned in, voice low enough for only his inner circle to hear. "Our father's plan rests on the very one who tried to destroy us, a being still bound to our enemy by love. Every fiber in my being tells me that this will not end with us all standing triumphant over our enemy. Keep on your guard and be ready to make a sudden adjustment to our plan if necessary."

He looks at each of them.

"Are you all with me?"

Simultaneously, they all nod, acknowledging and agreeing with Michael's stance.

"Good," Michael replies before returning to the crowd.

"Commanders!" he shouts, getting everyone's attention. "Gather your troops and meet me at the Light Barrier. We end this now."

Chapter
22

The War: Part i

At the Light Barrier, where God's radiance fades into the void, lies the Equilibrium, a thin line that divides good from evil.

On the one side lies hopes and dreams that are lined with gold reflecting light that holds every color that there can ever be. A realm of peace and unity that promises paradise for all who are within it. A world of purity that will never know disease or death.

Salvation

On the other side lies despair and nightmares wrought with chaos and corruption that form an everlasting darkness. A realm of war and selfishness that drives its inhabitants mad. A world of torment that tricks the mind into thinking that all is well.

Damnation.

It is in this fine line that hangs the very balance of life. This is the line that we walk during our worldly existence. It is why our inner darkness can so easily overcome us, but it is also why we can allow the light to bring us back.

And it is worth fighting for.

The Angelic Army stands at the ready just where the light begins to dim. The light forms rays as it reflects from the gold of their armor and weapons while their white robes sway underneath. The seven garrisons are lined up perfectly and equally spaced behind their leaders, who are standing directly in the center.

From left to right it is:

Gamaliel

Cassiel

Gabriel

Michael

Uriel

Raguel

Sariel

This also makes Michael the center of all garrisons.

He stares across the barrier at Caliban and Cronan. They are massive beings that are twice his height and three times his girth. A pale-yellow light shines through the Darkness that flows around them. Their mouths have been molded shut, and their faces look as though they were engraved from charred wood. Their eyes burn like large fire opals set aflame.

Large spines rise from their shoulders and backs while long, sharp razors extend out of their forearms and curl back beyond their elbows. Claws protrude from their fingers and toes.

Twisted reflections of the Archangels, Caliban and Cronan were no mere corrupted soldiers. They were the first Archdemons, Lilith's dark answer to God's chosen.

Behind them stood the rest of the lesser angels, all grouped together and eagerly awaiting the fight. Then there was what seemed like an endless sea of hounds all poised and ready to strike on command like trained attack dogs.

"We are ready when you are, Michael," Gamaliel says heavily, knowing what is about to unfold.

Michael, Uriel, and Gabriel all extend their right arm out to the ground and hold their hands open wide. They ignite their inner light and as they do so, angelic armor forms over their bodies. This armor consists of breast plates which had neck guards molded into them, gauntlets with angelic writing etched into them, leg plates, shin guards, and boots. All the armor was golden in color but lacked luster.

In their hands formed golden hilts that matched their gauntlets, and large pure light blades rose from them. They bring their hands together in front of their chests and clutch the swords tightly, causing the angelic inscriptions to light up in white, then they lower their arms to the side, swords on their right.

Michael turns his head and looks back at Uriel and Gabriel. A gold face plate now covers the left side of his face.

"I will take Caliban. The two of you handle Cronan." He turns around fully and looks at Gamaliel, Cassiel, Raguel, and Sariel. "You four lead the rest into battle. They have trained for this, and they are prepared, so I need you all to focus on the lesser angels if at all possible." He then looks out over the garrisons.

"To the Army of Light! You were created for this purpose, to drive back the Darkness and end its reign forever. Remember those who fell before you, the brothers and sisters who gave their light so ours could burn brighter. Let their memory guide your blades into battle!

The Darkness lies before you. Your enemy lies before you. They seek nothing else but to snuff out our Light. They do not care how or what matters need to be taken. They will fight dirty and without honor. And if we are to win this battle... we will need to be as merciless as they are.

WILL YOU BE MERCILESS?"

"YES!"

"WILL YOU FIGHT UNTIL YOUR DEATH?"

"YES"

"ARE YOU WITH ME?" Michael asks as he turns and charges the enemy.

Nothing but the roar of a rallied army can be heard behind him as the entire Army of Light charges to overtake the Dark Army.

The two armies clash in the asteroid field like a tsunami hitting the coastline. Bodies of both sides are thrown in the air. Hounds swarm over the angels in packs, successfully bringing many of them down while others are struck down before reaching their target.

The Original Four clammer with the troop of corrupted angels, taking many on at once. They maintain their own but still struggle with the unbalance in numbers, and try as they might, it is nearly impossible to focus on the corrupted angels alone.

They constantly have to dodge or avoid the fight going on around them. The hounds are everywhere, as well as angels, causing the four to be sidetracked and help out. To make matters worse, the corrupted angels care not who they fight, which makes it extremely hard for the four to keep their attention.

It doesn't take long for the battlefield to become blood-soaked and strewn with the dead. But the battle rages on.

Uriel and Gabriel attack Cronan in unison. He is a smart and formidable foe, using his size and strength to his advantage. They take turns striking him, but he makes use of his armor as he rips and claws at them. They too, have to deal with the occasional hound, and if an angel gets too close to Cronan, he tears them to pieces with ease before refocusing on the siblings.

Uniquely, Michael and Caliban battle away from the rest, unbothered by what is happening around them and able to focus solely on each other. Caliban easily has Michael on strength and durability, but Michael's quick mind and perceptive eye allow him to stand against his foe without hesitance.

Caliban swings with a wide right hook that Michael blocks with his sword. In turn, Caliban punches up towards Michael's stomach, but Michael plants his right hand on Caliban's arm and kicks him square in the jaw, sending Caliban off balance.

Michael goes in to continue the strike, but Caliban quickly regains himself and grabs Michael by the ankle, pulling him down and in as he punches downward at full force. Michael rolls his body to avoid the hit as it lands into the ground behind him. He kicks Caliban's wrist to break free of his grasp, but as he does so, Caliban kicks him in his lower back and sends him sliding across the dirt.

Michael stands up quickly, only to see Caliban leaping through the air and coming down with a two-handed hammer fist. Michael jumps back to avoid the hit, which causes an explosion of dirt and debris, blocking his view. Caliban leaps through the cloud and grabs Michael by the throat, then slams him down and starts dragging him across the ground.

Michael takes several blows to the head as this happens, but he swings his sword up and severs Caliban's left arm. Caliban stops immediately, grabs his arm, and Michael can hear muffled screaming coming from where Caliban's mouth should be. This shows Michael that Lilith had intentionally silenced them, yet another cruel form of torture.

Michael sees his opportunity and gets behind Caliban, but Caliban has turned primal and is clawing with his remaining arm as the other sprays blood all over. Michael dodges with practiced precision, waiting for the right moment to strike. He allows Caliban to get closer, and Caliban does exactly what Michael thought he would do. He rears up and draws back his good arm, leaving his front exposed, and Michael swiftly drives his sword through Caliban's jugular and out the back of his head.

Caliban falls limp to his knees, the remaining light within him flickering and fading as Michael withdraws his sword.

"Rest now, my brother," Michael whispered, lowering Caliban's ruined body with reverence. For a heartbeat, grief outweighed victory. "Your torment is over."

He looks over to see Gabriel kicking Cronan in the chest, causing him to stumble backward into Uriel's awaiting blade, and the sword pierces through his chest. He rears his head back in pain as he reaches to grab it with both hands. Uriel quickly pulls the sword out, spins around and decapitates Cronan, causing his light to fade instantly as his lifeless body hits the ground with a thud.

The three archangels look at each other to ensure that they are ok. Aside from some scratches and bruising, they are fine. They group together and look out across the carnage of the battlefield. The area is filled with the sounds of snarls and squeals mixed with yells and cries. Bodies of both armies lie dead and mangled throughout.

"MICHAEL!" Sariel shouts as he fends off hound after hound. "There's too many of them!"

Michael scans the field looking for any sign of God or Lucifer, but finds none. "Where are they?" he thinks to himself. He sees Gamaliel, Raguel, and Cassiel are struggling too, as are all the angels. Realizing he has no choice, he quickly turns to Gabriel and Uriel.

"Call all remaining garrisons to battle."

"All of them?" Gabriel responds hesitantly. "Even those protecting the Garden?"

"Gabriel, if we do not win this, there will not be a garden to protect. Our troops are getting slaughtered out there!"

Gabriel nods grimly. He pulls out a horn and blows into it, creating a long, low, and deep sound that echoes across space itself. He blows into it again, giving the signal for all of the angelic forces to come to battle. Hearing this causes many of the hounds to look up and tuck their ears back in fear and confusion.

It doesn't take long for a sea of white and gold to appear, containing nearly five hundred thousand additional reinforcements.

Just as they are about to join the battle, Lilith's shrill shriek shoots across the battlefield, causing all who remain to fall still and look up to find her looking down on them like a hawk searching for prey. She scans the field until she and Michael lock eyes. Slowly, she floats down, landing softly on her feet in front of him. The forces of Light and Dark fall back behind their respected leaders, distancing themselves from what surely will be a hard-fought battle.

"Where is he?" she asks. "Where is Lucifer?"

Michael remains silent as he stares down at her.

"You can drop the tough act, Michael; you know that you cannot defeat me." She looks behind him. "Even with your brother and sister behind you."

"You may be right," Michael says. "But we will surely try."

Without saying a word, Lilith reaches up, twists her wrist and snaps in the same motion.

Instantaneously, the entire Dark Army falls flat and turns back into the Darkness. With another flick of her hand, it rises up and ensnares every member of the angelic army.

With a downward motion, Lilith clenched the battlefield in her grasp. Darkness coiled and crushed, and in an instant, the Light of thousands winked out, leaving only Michael, Gabriel, Uriel, and the original four writhing in her snare. The remaining seven are not without pain, however. Their Light is significantly stronger than the others but the Darkness acts as poison, burning away at their skin causing them all to cry out in agony.

Michael is shocked by the extent of Lilith's power. It was more than he had imagined that it could be. Her control over the Darkness was horrifying to say the least. If she had been able to do this all along, why hadn't she done it before now he thinks to himself while fighting to stay alive in her snare.

"That is enough!" comes God's booming voice.

Lilith looks over to see God standing a few yards away from her.

"Where. Is. Lucifer?" she snarls.

"I am here."

Lilith spins around quickly to see Lucifer standing directly behind her. She looks at him in surprised shock as if she was seeing a ghost. Lucifer reaches up and cups her cheek with his hand.

"There is no longer a need to fight, my love," he says gently to her. "We can return to our garden and make it whole again. We can leave and live out the rest of our days in peace far away from here, never to be bothered again." He brings his forehead to hers. "We can start a family."

Lilith pulls back in disgust. "Start a family?! We had a family, and they took it from us!"

"Yes, they did." Lucifer snaps back. "And I am not saying that we forget that. But Lilith, we have an eternity ahead of us. We should not let a single moment in time dictate the rest of our lives."

"A single moment in time? Is that all it was to you?! Lucifer, you are a fool to believe that they would leave us alone. Especially as we are now."

"God's only enemy is the Darkness. He only seeks to wipe it from existence, not us. He has promised me that if you allow the Darkness to be purged from you, he will let us go."

"And you believe him?!"

"Yes, I do."

Hearing this causes Lilith to shake her head in disagreement. "Why?"

Lucifer takes Lilith's hands into his own. "I cannot tell you why, I just need you to trust me.

Lilith turns and looks at God before turning back to Lucifer. "What has he done to you?"

Lucifer shakes his head. "Lilith, please, don't do this."

Lilith stares at him coldly. "If you want me to go with you," she points at God. "His life is the price."

Lucifer looks over at God. He has thought about ending his life since that day in the garden. Then he looks back into Lilith's eyes and is taken back to the time that they first met his.

He reaches up and brushes a strand of hair from her face. "I am sorry, but I will not fight him. I will not risk losing you again." He says as he allows the Darkness to enter, transforming him into his devilish form.

"Silly boy." Lilith sneers as Lucifer's body begins to seize as it had done before when he crossed the Light Barrier. Lucifer looks down to see Lilith twisting her hand down by her waist. "The Darkness chose me as its champion; you are but a pawn in the game. A puppet to be controlled by my strings."

God's eyes widen in fear as he realizes the trap that he has just fallen into.

"And now you will kill your siblings as I deal with your father," she says as Lucifer falls under her spell. His eyes turn red, and embers begin rising from his skin. She caresses his hair then down his cheek before turning around and facing God, an evil smile spread across her face.

"Shall we begin?"

The War: Part ii

A strong wind has begun blowing that is causing Lucifer's hair to whip across his face while he stares coldly at his brothers and sisters as they struggle to free themselves. The other four have already passed out from the pain, barely clinging to life.

He turns and looks at the fight going on between Lilith and God. Lilith is decimating God in hand-to-hand combat. As fast as God is, she is faster and is landing every blow. To God's credit, he is holding his own and landing a few counterstrikes, but he has had to become more defensive as Lilith's wrath ensued.

Michael locked eyes with his fallen brother, masking agony behind steel resolve. In that stare lingered defiance, grief, and memory of who they once were.

"So, this is how it ends, is it? You are doing her bidding and slaughtering us as we are bound?"

"As was I while my family was murdered." Lucifer sneers back.

"We were not the ones who did those things, Lucifer."

"Satan." Lucifer snaps. "Lucifer is gone now. And even so, you did nothing to stop it."

Michael looks over to the fight happening in the distance. God is strong, but he will not last much longer. He needs his help. His Light has started to dim and return after each hit. A sure sign that his power has begun to drain.

He turns back to his fallen brother. "Then release me and let's do this properly."

A smirk forms on Satan's face as he folds his arms. He leans in slightly before saying, "I accept your challenge, but know that when you fall, your last sight will be of Gabriel and Uriel's heads at your feet." Then he waves his hand, freeing Michael from his restraints.

Michael rises slowly and looks at his brother and sister. "Hold on," he mutters to them. He bends down to pick up his sword, but his fallen brother stops him.

"No," Lucifer growled. "No blades, no light. Hand to hand. Brother against brother."

Again, Michael stands up straight and locks eyes. "As you wish." Then he strips his armor off as well as the top portion of his robe, paying tribute to his late brother Raphael.

The estranged brothers begin to circle each other, poised and ready to attack. Satan is the first to strike. He closes the gap between them with incredible speed and lands a three-strike combination. First to Michael's stomach, then two to his face.

Michael winces in pain but recovers quickly, blocking Satan's next strike before delivering his own. He kicks his opponent's left knee, causing him to stagger as he delivers his left fist square into Satan's nose.

Satan takes a step back, laughing as he does so. "Okay little brother, well done." He then charges in for another strike but dips low at the last second, negating Michael's defense. He wraps his arms around Michael's waist and tackles him to the ground.

The two wrestle on the ground trading blows and alternating control. Blood smeared across their faces, streaking onto each other as they grappled in the dirt. Michael grabs Satan around his waist and begins to lift him up. Satan rains down elbows trying to cause Michael to drop him, but Michael endures. He arches his back and brings Satan over his head, slamming him down face first into the dirt behind them.

The force of the hit causes Satan to bounce up and tumble away. He regains his footing, but Michael is right there with a knee to his face. His head snaps to the side but he uses the momentum to spin around and trip Michael. He mounts him and begins choking him with both hands.

"YOU WERE MY BROTHER!!!" He shouts down at him. "WE WERE MEANT TO PROTECT ONE ANOTHER!!!"

Michael pried the hands from his throat just enough to gasp, "You chose her over us, over our father, over everything we built!"

Michael brings his knees up and pushes Satan off of him. As he lands, he is met with a blow from Michael's wing that hits him in the jaw, causing him to be knocked to the ground. Michael charges him again but he throws an uppercut and connects to the bottom of Michael's jaw, sending him flying up and backwards.

Michael lands hard on his back. He sees his father still fighting with Lilith. God's Light has begun to flicker after each hit. A sure sign that he was almost out of energy. He knows that if he doesn't help God soon, they will all be lost. He rolls over and looks at his brother who is knelt down and breathing heavily. Then over to Gabriel and Uriel, who are also starting to fade.

He sits up and hangs his head, knowing that he only has one option left. Disappointed in himself that it has had to come to this.

Michael's chest heaved as he weighed the cost of silence. At last, through broken breaths, he forced the words: 'If she wins... your child dies.'.

Satan looks over to him with confusion in his eyes.

"If she wins, your child dies," Michael says again, more clearly.

Satan straightens his posture and looks at Michael.

"What did you say?"

"I saved it," Michael says through his pain. "I saved it that day in the garden."

Gabriel and Uriel's eyes shoot over to Michael. Their astonishment as to what he was confessing being stronger than their pain at that moment.

The devil shares this shock and has begun to hover over to Micheal, his head tilted slightly, and brow furrowed as he seeks clarification.

"Speak plainly."

Michael looks over to God again. "I found the stillborn child under the apple tree before we left the garden that day. As God and the others flew away, I picked it up and hid it within my robe. I've kept it hidden for years, thinking that one day it might bring an answer to all this."

"You lie," Satan says as he turns towards his other two siblings.

"I do not," Michael says while grimacing. "Despite what went on that day, you were still my brother, and I could not just let you go. The child was the only piece of you that was left."

He looks up to see that Satan's eyes have returned to blue.

"Is it intact?" he asks pleadingly.

"Its body is. But I fear that its soul remained in your garden as Lilith's had."

A memory seared across Lucifer's mind, the faint cry he had once heard in the garden. Then, he had dismissed it as a trick of silence. Now, it pulsed with new meaning, a fragile thread of hope. "You speak the truth?" he asks.

"Yes, Brother, I do." Michael pauses briefly. "But if she wins, he will never live. All souls are connected to God's Light, and if he dies, they all will die as well. The child and her."

Lucifer looks over at Lilith.

"Release us so that we can stop her and end this peacefully."

Lucifer turns back to Michael. "I cannot handle yet another betrayal, Michael."

"He's telling the truth, Lucifer," Gabriel calls over through his pain. "We've seen it."

Lucifer's mind races as he searches for the right move to make. If his siblings are indeed telling the truth, this could be what is needed to end this war.

'I will release you,' Lucifer declared, his voice cutting through the battlefield, 'but Lilith is mine to face."

And with a snap of his fingers, he releases his siblings. "Go," he commands before flying off to stop Lilith.

The War: Part iii

Lilith has significantly damaged God. With each strike that she delivers, his Light diminishes. Her power swelled with every strike, feeding on the Light she stripped from God. A purple aurora has started glowing just above her skin as she consumes the Light God is losing. She lands blow after blow, watching as God struggles to keep at it.

Finally, God begins to fade in and out, unable to keep his guard up. Lilith's punches continue to rain on him, and she is laughing manically now as her victory draws near.

"You will feel as helpless as I was that day!" She screams, hitting him again.

"You will watch as I drain the light from your children."

Another blow.

She grabs God by the face and pulls him in close. "And then I will kill you as merciless as you killed my child."

She draws back to deliver the knockout blow, but just as she is about to throw the punch, a hand grabs her arm, causing her head to spin around and look Lucifer in the eyes. She looks at him in a confused frustration.

"What are you doing?!" she snarls as she rips her arm from his grasp.

She turns around to hit God, but again she is stopped by Lucifer. This time, he has turned her around and is now holding her by the shoulders and looking deep into her eyes.

Anger courses through her veins as she once again shakes loose of Lucifer's grip. It is only then that she notices that his eyes have returned to their natural blue state. She looks behind him and sees that Michael, Gabriel, and Uriel have gone missing and pieces it all together.

"You dare betray me again?!" she growls.

"Lilith, listen to me."

"NO! I am tired of words. I am tired of the back and forth. It is clear to me now that you will never understand my affliction! If you want to choose them over me, so be it." She levitates high and unleashes the power she has gained. "I will kill you all."

And without giving Lucifer a chance to say another word, bursts of energy begin to shoot through air. Lucifer quickly picks God up and shelters them both behind a large rock.

"What is that?!" Lucifer asks God.

"That is the full power of the Darkness," God replies in disbelief.

"How do we stop it?"

God shakes his head defeatedly. "We can't."

The bursts of energy land all around them. As they land on the bodies left from the war, it instantly decays and reduces them to ash. Lucifer looks on in fear as Lilith continues to be blinded by her rage. If he was being honest with himself, he wasn't sure it was even her in there anymore.

He turns and looks off into the distance. "They need to hurry." He mutters softly.

God hears this and looks at him, puzzled. "Who?"

Lucifer looks at God for the first time without a thought of killing him crossing his mind. For the first time since that day in the garden, Lucifer's hatred wavered. He no longer saw the tyrant who cast him down, but the father he once adored. He places his hand on God's shoulder and squeezes it.

"If I don't make it back." He pauses as he gently shakes God and struggles to not let his voice crack. "Know that I love you."

God's confusion renders him unable to respond quick enough before Lucifer stands up and begins walking towards Lilith. All he can do is watch as his firstborn son walks bravely into the storm, seemingly unfazed by the danger around him.

Though he had to dodge a few of the energy bursts, Lucifer was able to walk right up to Lilith. Her eyes are wide and burn brightly, but her face is emotionless. He is confident now that she has given up her control of the Darkness and is allowing it to run rampant as it was intended.

The force of the energy spiraling around is almost unbearable, but he doesn't waver. Slowly, his feet lift from the ground as he hovers up to Lilith and forces himself into the core of the storm.

"Lilith," he says gently as he cups her face in his hands. "Lilith, come back to me."

But Lilith remains unresponsive.

Even though it causes him great pain, he leans in and presses his forehead to hers. "Come back to me," he pleads gently. "They have our son."

Lilith's eyes go from a lifeless stare to a sense of awareness. She starts to blink rapidly as she regains focus. Once she does, all she can see are the eyes of the one that she once loved.

The eyes of the one that she still loves.

"They have our son," Lucifer whispered again. The words struck deeper than any blade, pulling Lilith's mind back from the abyss until her fury faltered and her power wavered.

"That isn't possible," she says brokenheartedly as the storm subsides.

Lucifer's eyes begin to water. "No... the other one."

Lilith blinks hard as she tries to understand what is being said to her. But all she can feel is doubt.

"They lie."

"Not this time," Lucifer says as he motions for Lilith to look behind her.

She turns around to find Michael, Uriel, and Gabriel all standing together peacefully. Michael is cradling something in his arms that is wrapped in a soft cloth blanket.

Lilith's eyes grow wide as she looks from the blanket up to Michael. "Is that...?"

Michael pulls the blanket down and reveals that it is indeed the stillborn child, perfectly intact and looking exactly like it had the day it was pulled from her womb.

Lilith instantly stops her crusade, drops to her knees, and cups her mouth as she tries to hold back from crying. Lucifer comes up behind her and places his hand on her shoulder.

"What you see is only its body; his soul lies somewhere in our garden. In exchange for God's life, they have agreed to give us our son and let us leave."

Lilith's anger starts to grow once more as she turns to face Lucifer. "In exchange for what? Peace? Come now Lucifer, you cannot believe that they will allow us to live in peace with a Nephilim." She turns back around. "Give me the child and I will end you all quickly and without pain."

Lucifer puts himself between Lilith and the others.

"If you snuff out God's light, we will never feel the warmth of our son's." he says somberly. "All souls are connected to God's light, including yours. If he dies, so does everything else."

Lilith stares at Lucifer, soaking in everything that has brought them to this point. She hasn't noticed that Michael has come up beside her until he speaks to her.

"You were wronged that day," he says as he places the child in Lilith's arms, causing her to look at him in shock. "I hope that this rights that wrong in some way." He gently rubs the head of the child, then looks Lilith in the eye.

They stare at each other for a moment. She can see that Michael is sincere in his words. She then looks down at the child in her arms. He looks so peaceful, as if he is sleeping. Her heart that has been so cold and set on revenge now pumps warmth throughout her body as joy fills her.

The Darkness drained from her like ink seeping into water. Her skin brightened, her form softened, and before them stood once more the radiant woman she had been. She holds the child tight and brings her head down to its own, and the tears begin to flow. Lucifer wraps them both in his arms and starts to cry as well.

He then looks over at Michael and the others. He lets go of Lilith and hovers over to them, coming to a stop a few feet in front of Michael. A period of silence takes place as he awkwardly tries to come up with something to say. Finally, he thinks of something.

"I cannot undo the sins of my past, nor she, hers. I will not apologize for the actions that I have taken, but I do regret some of them." He pauses to see if anyone else wants to speak, but when no one does, he continues. "I will bear the burden of keeping the Darkness within me and honor my word of secluding ourselves, never to be seen or bothered again, as long as you all can honor your word of leaving us be."

He looks to each of them, awaiting a response. Michael turns and looks at Uriel and Gabriel before turning back to Lucifer.

"You have our word."

Lucifer inhales deeply. As he does so, he spreads his arms wide, and all of The Darkness swirls around him. It pulls from every direction, causing Lucifer to become larger and even more menacing-looking. His horns grow wider, longer, and more mangled. His body begins to resemble one of the shadow creatures with long arms and shorter dog-like legs, except far more muscular and horrific. A short snout now rests on his face with razor teeth and a forked tongue. Large smokey wings sprout from his back and stretch fully extended. However, despite this new beast form, Lucifer's eyes have remained the same ice blue indicating that he was still in control of it all.

"Are you still with us?" Michael asks just to be sure.

Lucifer's eyes shift over to look at Michael, but he does not move. Instead, he looks at his new features and examines what has become of him. His hands are massive with sharp claws. Large, jagged spines extend from his elbows, and a long, dragon-like tail has formed out of his lower back.

Eventually, he turns to Michael. But before he can say anything, a quick burst of light flashes behind Lucifer and causes them all to look to see what it was.

Lilith is facing them, still cradling the child but her eyes have gone wide and her jaw agape. A dark orange glow is coming from within her chest.

"Lucifer..." she says just before collapsing.

Behind her stands God, blazing with full radiance, a small orb cradled in his palm. His eyes locked on Lucifer and as his fingers closed, the orb shattered. Lilith's soul splintered with it.

For a single moment, silence falls as everyone registers their own feelings as to what just took place.

That silence is broken as Lucifer begins to take quick deep breaths. His shock turns to anger then to rage. His eyes turn amber as he lets out the most primal of roars and charges toward God. God instantly teleports away from him and extends his arms straight out to the sides. All the remaining stars begin to dim as God's light grows brighter.

The three siblings look on in shock as Lucifer tries to catch God as he continues to teleport randomly until he lands on a large asteroid, and all the stars go dark, including Sanctuarium. This causes Lucifer to stop his pursuit and look around. The only source of Light in all the cosmos was stemming from God, who now had a new form of his own.

His body was pure white with no distinguishing features, almost mannequin like. He had no mouth, ears, or nostrils. His pale-yellow eyes took up the whole socket and were shooting flames from them. He was covered in hard light armor that looked as though it had been chiseled out of diamonds, and streaks of electricity swarmed around him, occasionally bolting off on their own.

Aside from the armor, Lucifer was the only one to ever see God like this. This was the God that had awoken to destroy the Darkness. This was God at his full glory. But this was not the Darkness that God had been tasked with. This was Lucifer's Darkness, and he had been betrayed by God for the last time.

Calmly and slowly, Lucifer begins to walk towards God, his hulking body creating burning footprints as he goes. He reaches an unwavering God and looks down at him. Lucifer is easily six feet taller than God now, yet God stands confidently as he looks up to him.

A tense stare down ensues as the unstoppable force stands toe-to-toe with the immovable object.

Finally, Lucifer flexes his entire body as he bends down to God's level and releases that primal roar in God's face, thus signaling the beginning of the battle between father and son. Between God and the Devil.

Chapter
23

The Beginning of the End

Michael, Uriel, and Gabriel can do nothing but stand by and watch as the two titans collide. Though smaller in size, God moved with unmatched agility, weaving through Lucifer's furious blows. However, Lucifer was relentless in his attacks, slashing, clawing, and snapping all in a fury. Anything that he could do to get to God, he was trying.

But God is nothing if not patient. Carelessly he avoids Lucifer's strikes while waiting for the time to strike himself. However, Lucifer gives no chance of attack with the way he is moving.

"Does he not tire?" God thinks to himself as the two of them use the entire asteroid as their arena.

"You cannot run forever!" Lucifer snarls.

God stays silent as he continues to avoid Lucifer's blows.

"Fight me, you coward!" Lucifer yells in frustration.

God knows that he is not strong enough to fight Lucifer in hand-to-hand combat. Measured as a whole, they were all but equals, but the Darkness still acted as a poison to him, which gave Lucifer the advantage.

Suddenly, Lucifer makes an unexpected move. He stops chasing God and comes to a complete halt. The two stare each other down until Lucifer snorts before turning his head and looking at Michael and the others, then back to God.

"If you will not fight me willingly, then I will force you to," he says as he begins walking toward his siblings.

A cold chill shoots through God's entire body as he realizes the position that he is in. He either stands by and watches his children get slaughtered or he fights Lucifer leading to a certain death. It is nearly the same ultimatum that he put Lucifer in all those years ago.

"Michael," God calls out telepathically.

"Yes Father?" Michael responds emotionlessly as he watches Lucifer getting closer.

"Michael, you have to take your brother and sister and get as far away from here as possible."

"Yes, Michael," Lucifer's gruff voice interrupts, shocking them both that he can hear their thoughts. "Run, little brother. Run as our coward of a father always has. Tell yourselves there is hope after I snuff out the light of God. Do as he has done and fill the others with false hopes and dreams that you have no power to fulfill."

He stops walking and begins to speak aloud for all to hear.

"Do you all not yet see that he is not the Almighty? That he does not have the strength to defeat the Darkness? He is not God!" He levitates himself off the ground. "I AM!"

Veins of orange glow from inside and spread throughout his body like fresh magma through rock. His eyes set ablaze in white fire, and embers spew from the heat escaping from his lungs, causing sparks to shoot from his mouth as he speaks.

Seeing his moment, God instantly transitions himself under Lucifer and delivers a powerful upper cut that sends Lucifer spiraling. Before he has a chance to regain his composure, God is on him again. God is landing every strike. As he hits Lucifer in one direction, it is immediately followed up with another blow that sends him in the other direction. God plants his hands on the ground and kicks Lucifer under the jaw with both feet, snapping his head back with a sickening crunch.

But Lucifer withstands the blow and grabs God by his ankles, then turns and swings him over his shoulder and slams him into the ground, creating a crater and sending a shockwave so hard that it nearly knocks the archangels off their feet. He reaches down and picks God up by his throat and brings him to eye level before head-butting him so hard that his light flickers.

A smile forms across Lucifer's twisted face. He rears back to head-butt God again, but an arm around his own throat causes him to stop. He turns the best that he can to see that Michael, in great pain, is trying to choke him out.

The Darkness was like pure radiation to Michael, but he had no choice but to help his father. He squeezes Lucifer's neck with all his might as Lucifer tears away at his arm and back like a fresh razor through paper. The pain is all but unbearable but still Michael presses on.

Suddenly, Uriel swoops in and tackles Lucifer from the side, sending them all to the ground and causing Lucifer to release God, yet Michael stays locked around his neck. As Lucifer stands up, Uriel grabs his right wrist while Gabriel grabs the other, and they stretch him out, trying to hold him at bay in order to give Michael some relief.

But it is short-lived.

With terrifying strength, Lucifer yanked them together, smashing their skulls before they had time to react. Uriel and Gabriel collide into one another's heads so hard that they are instantly knocked unconscious and fall to the ground. He then reaches up to Michael and grabs both wings, one in each hand. He starts pulling hard, causing such pain that Michael is forced to let go or have his wings torn off.

Lucifer brings his defeated and bloodied brother in front of him and turns him so that he can look him in the eye, holding Michael by the top of his head in his left hand.

Calmly, Lucifer speaks. "If you would have stayed out of this, I would have allowed you all to live. We could have started anew and built our own world. But your loyalty to the false god has sealed your fate."

He reaches behind Michael and grabs his left wing at the base.

"You will never understand the agony of watching life drain from your child... but you will feel my suffering."

With that statement, he slowly begins to tear Michael's wing off.

Michael screams in agony as he struggles to free himself, but Lucifer's grip is too strong.

The screams of his son snap God from his daze and he looks over in horror at the sight. Uriel and Gabriel lay at the Beast's feet, burning away from the Darkness radiation. Michael is writhing in agony and clawing away at Lucifer.

"LUCIFER!"

Lucifer stops torturing Michael and turns to look at God.

"Put. Him. Down."

Lucifer drops Michael causing him to hit the ground with a heavy thud. The mightiest angel lies defeated in a slump, his flesh shredded and burned. His wing near completely torn from his back. With significant effort he lifts his head enough to see Lucifer walking over to God before he passes out from pain and exhaustion.

"I am sorry, my children," God says heavily to himself. "But I need to borrow your light." He then reaches out and pulls the remaining life force from the three archangels, returning him to his full power. "Please forgive me."

Lucifer reaches God's location and towers over him as a familiar silence falls around them.

"No more running. No more pleading or negotiating. We do not stop until one of us dies." Lucifer growls.

God's cold and silent stare gives Lucifer his answer.

With that, the two leap off the asteroid and engage in battle once more.

They speed through space, causing cosmic events each time they collide. It doesn't take long before all the universe is littered with new stars. Stars made from the sheer force of the compressed energies of Light and Dark, enabling them to ignite and burn constantly.

Lucifer once again is the primary attacker and is able to land several blows. But what he didn't know was that he was falling right into God's trap. The more stars that were made, the weaker Lucifer was becoming. Eventually, he found himself surrounded by giant balls of light, and a containment of his own creation, though he had not yet realized it.

On and on he attacks, still blinded by his rage, but slowly he begins to notice that his strikes are not having the same effect on God as they had before. Instead, God had become more offensive, now trading blow for blow. Soon Lucifer was forced to switch purely to defense as God ramped up his attack.

He hits Lucifer so hard that it sends him spiraling like a comet entering the atmosphere. He follows up with another strike equal to the first, then another and another. With each hit, they pick up speed until the Forsaken Garden begins to come into view.

Seeing this, Lucifer realizes God's plan. He attempts to avoid God's next strike by rolling out of the way, but God sees this move and counteracts it. As Lucifer rolls to the side, God grabs his waist from behind and starts hurling them both to the barren land mass.

Lucifer uses all the strength that he has left trying to break free from God's grip. He throws his elbows down, attempting to stab God with the razor-like spines that protrude from them. He rips at God's arms and hands in hopes of forcing a release. But even in the great pain that is being caused, God holds on strong.

Lucifer looks up just in time to see the ground close in on him.

The two titans hit the garden with such force that it shatters it into millions of pieces. The shockwave is so strong that it causes a nearby star to collapse in on itself, triggering a supernova and thus, a black hole.

The black hole is vicious and immediately starts to consume all that is around it creating a storm of immeasurable strength.

God has returned to his humanoid form and stands over a defeated Lucifer on a small fragment of the garden. He is holding his right shoulder where Lucifer had landed a lucky strike just before they hit. A thick black ooze drips from the wound and through God's fingers.

The gravitational pull from the black hole has created hurricane-like winds, causing the smaller fragments to whip past them.

Lucifer only has enough strength to rise to his knees. He has transformed from the beast back to his devil form. His hair blows aggressively in the wind like tiny whips slapping his face. He takes in the sight of the black hole and his father's eclipsed silhouette before it. He knows that he has been defeated.

"I have no need for one of your lectures," he scoffs. "Kill me and be done with it."

God turns and removes his hand from his wound and places it on Lucifer's shoulder. Instantly, the vision of the perfect garden enters Lucifer's brain, and the two of them are no longer on the small floating rock, but instead they are in the garden as if they had stepped into a dream.

"How?" Lucifer asks as he feels the warmth of the sun on his face.

"This garden is more beautiful than anything either of us could create alone," God says as he reaches down and touches a rose. "But if you will notice, the colors are not as bright as they are in the other gardens. They are darker and more grounded, more... natural."

Lucifer looks around and realizes that God is telling the truth. He places his hand on the trunk of a tree that is next to him. To his surprise, he feels the presence of both Light and Dark flowing from within. Slowly he turns his head and eyes over to God for an answer.

God turns and looks across the horizon of the Garden and begins to explain. "Before your creation, I fought the Darkness alone for longer than I can remember. During that time, I began to gain knowledge of a time before this universe existed and learned that I was indeed created myself for the sole purpose of defeating the Darkness and returning everything to how it was before.

Failed attempt after failed attempt, I could not win the battle, only delay it. And that is when it occurred to me that in order to fulfill my duty, I had to begin where it ended. Where the Light and Dark existed together in unison."

He turns and looks at Lucifer.

"I needed balance," God says.

As he says this, the garden whisks away like dust in the wind, and they are back in the Forbidden Garden.

"My creators were able to contain the Darkness. And that is what I need to do as well."

Lucifer's mind begins to race as he puts together the pieces of the puzzle God has laid before him.

"You knew this was going to happen," he says as it all begins to make sense. "No. You intended for this all to happen."

God looks down at him. His hand is still on Lucifer's shoulder.

"The Darkness cannot be destroyed, only contained." He says as he begins to pull what is left of the Light out of Lucifer. I knew that the only thing that could contain it would be a vessel made of everything that the Light was not. This plan was set in motion before your creation. I shaped you. Molded you into what I needed. I purposely chose your Garden above the others. I purposely made the man infertile. I purposely made the woman corrupt you. I laid the path to your true purpose of creation, and you walked it perfectly, unaware of it all."

God kneels to look Lucifer eye to eye.

"Every step of your life was shaped by my hand, every trial designed to forge you into a vessel strong enough to contain the Darkness. And you did not disappoint."

The last of Lucifer's light drains into God's hand.

"And now the Darkness relies on you as its life force as you do it. One cannot be without the other. You will be imprisoned again while I use you to create a new universe in perfect balance."

Horror forms over Lucifer's face as he realizes the fate bestowed upon him, but it is quickly replaced by laughter.

"If what you say is true, this prison will not hold me forever."

"I know," God says, causing Lucifer's smile to fade.

All other traces of the Forsaken Garden have been pulled into the black hole, leaving only the fragment they are on to remain. God stands up and starts to hover, causing the rock to begin getting sucked in.

Lucifer never breaks eye contact with God as everything around him fades to black, leaving only the color of his eyes to pierce through. Right before he disappears, he sends a final message to his father with hatred in his voice.

"Though fallen I have become, through Hell I shall rise again."

Author's Note

Thank you all for taking the time to read my first book. I have been working on this project on and off since 2011. The basis of this story all came from a single question that I feel has never been given a solid answer.

The question of "why?"

Why did Lucifer really fall from the grace of God?

Being raised in a religion that failed to provide a suitable explanation, I sought out other religions to see if they could provide a better answer. And though I gained more knowledge on the subject, the answer to my question still eluded me.

It seemed as though that the only answer to my question was the same as where God came from, it just simply was that way and that was not a satisfactory answer to me.

So, I came up with my own.

Keep in mind that this is not my belief, it is just something that I believe makes a good story.

I originally had planned on only writing one book; however, as a lifelong fan of the science fiction genre, I did not want to leave my readers in the same dilemma that I was in, which was wondering why this all happened and what happens next.

The idea for this book, and its upcoming sequels, has been derived from my fascination with movies, video games, anime, and of course, other books. I love a good "Ah Ha!" moment as well as a good "Oh Shit…" moment.

I aimed to be vivid enough that most readers see what I see, while still leaving space to imagine. So, I tried to describe everything in a way that everyone would get a relatively close idea of seeing things exactly how I intended them, while still leaving room for you to imagine on your own, and I hope that I have achieved that.

This book is shorter than most sci-fi for two reasons.

First, most readers know the Heaven-versus-Hell arc; I focused on the twist rather than retelling the familiar. Having you waste your time reading things that you already know would have only led to boredom.

Two, this is an origin story. It is meant to set the scene and give a back story for the larger tale that is to come. I didn't want to cram unnecessary things into it simply just for the sake of a word count.

At the time of writing this, I do not know what the future holds for this tale, but one thing is certain. No matter the outcome, I have completed a dream of mine to write a book and share a story. And if I can inspire one person to do the same, then I would feel that I have achieved what I've set out to achieve. Your biggest enemy is yourself. Take the risk, step out of your comfort zone, and you may open a door to a world of opportunity.

In closing, I would like to thank you again for taking the time to not only read the story but also for reading this note. I hope that it gave you some insight, but more importantly, I hope that my writings have brought some form of joy into your life, and I look forward to taking many more journeys together.

Best wishes,

Eric Adams

Epilogue

"Michael. Michael wake up."

God's voice resonated in Michael's mind. He blinked, and the familiar sight of Sanctuarium snapped into focus. He tries to form words but is too confused to do so.

God sees this and presses a finger to his own lips. "I'll answer everything," God said, weariness in his tone, "but first, you must answer me." He then points over to a large cylinder container with tubes running from it. "What is this?"

Within the container lies the body of a sleeping angel floating in pure water. But this angel is different. Its long hair is jet black, and its wings are feathered like a crow. It has a muscular body with a skin color that looks like Death had touched it. Yet somehow, it was familiar to God.

"Is that who I think it is?"

"No," Michael replies emotionally. "But he is a part of it."

"A part?"

Michael knows that there is no escaping the conversation and decides to just come clean.

"It's his body," Michael said, "housing the stillborn's soul."

God shoots him an angry glance, then takes a deep breath before asking, "Is this how you were able to achieve all that you had?"

"Yes."

God ponders for a moment. "You should not have hidden this from me." God's gaze softened a fraction. "But it may yet serve a purpose. Have you given it a name?"

"Yes."

"What is it?"

"Azrael."